"I'm Not Really Married,"

Catherine told Jake as they drove away from the wedding hall.

"Expensive rehearsal, don't you think?"

Catherine shot him an exasperated look, ripped off her veil and tossed it in the back seat. "You know what I mean...." Her voice trailed off as she turned away. "No consummation, no marriage. Besides, we never completed the paperwork."

Just then, a convertible full of teenage girls pulled alongside. Noticing Catherine in her wedding dress and Jake in the one suit he owned, they started honking the horn, tapping keys against soda cans in the familiar symbolic gesture and blowing kisses at what they assumed were newlyweds. Catherine slumped in her seat and groaned, and for just one crazy second, Jake wanted to plant one heck of a kiss on the bride....

Dear Reader,

Can you believe that for the next three months we'll be celebrating the publication of the 1000th Silhouette Desire? That's quite a milestone! The festivities begin this month with six books by some of your longtime favorites and exciting new names in romance.

We'll continue into next month, May, with the actual publication of Book #1000—by Diana Palmer—and then we'll keep the fun going into June. There's just so much going on that I can't put it all into one letter. You'll just have to keep reading!

This month we have an absolutely terrific lineup, beginning with *Saddle Up*, a MAN OF THE MONTH by Mary Lynn Baxter. There's also *The Groom, I Presume?*—the latest in Annette Broadrick's DAUGHTERS OF TEXAS miniseries. *Father of the Brat* launches the new FROM HERE TO PATERNITY miniseries by Elizabeth Bevarly, and *Forgotten Vows* by Modean Moon is the first of three books about what happens on THE WEDDING NIGHT. Lass Small brings us her very own delightful sense of humor in *A Stranger in Texas*. And our DEBUT AUTHOR this month is Anne Eames with *Two Weddings and a Bride*.

And next month, as promised, Book #1000, a MAN OF THE MONTH, *Man of Ice* by Diana Palmer!

Lucia Macro,
Senior Editor

Please address questions and book requests to:
Silhouette Reader Service
U.S.: 3010 Walden Ave., P.O. Box 1325, Buffalo, NY 14269
Canadian: P.O. Box 609, Fort Erie, Ont. L2A 5X3

ANNE EAMES
TWO WEDDINGS
AND A BRIDE

SILHOUETTE *Desire*®
™ Published by Silhouette Books
America's Publisher of Contemporary Romance

With thanks and appreciation to my insightful editor, Melissa Senate,
and to all my RWA friends, especially fellow critiquers
Jeanne Couzens, Corky Conrad and Fran Krauss, as well as to authors
who generously shared their time and "secrets"—Shelly Thacker,
Ruth Ryan Langan, Kate Hoffmann and my own personal guardian
angel, Lucy Taylor. Special thanks to my tolerant and sexy husband,
Bill, who learned to cook, put up with my odd hours and moods, and
helped research a few particular scenes. Hugs and kisses all around!

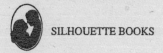 SILHOUETTE BOOKS

ISBN 0-373-05996-5

TWO WEDDINGS AND A BRIDE

Printed in U.S.A.

ANNE EAMES

has a varied background, including managing a theater, a bridal salon, and a constuction association, netting several marketing and communications awards along the way. In 1991 she joined the Romance Writers of America, later becoming a Golden Heart finalist, the winner of the Maggie Award, and, finally, a published author—her lifelong dream.

Anne and her engineer husband, Bill, live in Southeastern Michigan and share a family of five—two hers (Tim and Tom), two his (Erin and David), and one theirs (an adorable miniature dachshund, Punkin).

Dear Reader,

There you are! I'm glad I finally found you—and vice versa. After a lifetime of *dreaming* about sharing my stories with you, I decided we'd meet a lot quicker if I wrote them down. Last summer I visited New York and a clairvoyant named Zena told me if I applied myself, in 1996 I'd exceed my expectations. I didn't want my friends and family thinking I was crazy plopping down cash for Zena or that she might be wrong, so I wrote like a banshee and voilà, *Two Weddings and a Bride* won the coveted Maggie award and shortly after was snatched up by Silhouette Desire. Six weeks later Desire bought my second book, and I'm hard at work on a third. Now I find myself driving down the freeway engrossed in my stories, missing exits and, too often, nearly rear-ending the car in front of me.

The fact that *Two Weddings and a Bride* is part of Desire's **Celebration 1000** makes this debut experience a doubly exciting one for me. I hope the following pages bring a smile to your face, an occasional tear to your eye, the need for an oscillating fan.

My next story, *You're What?!*, will take you on a Caribbean cruise where my heroine meets her Mr. Right— just hours after she's artificially inseminated. Watch for *You're What?!* late summer.

I'd love to hear from you, whether you'd like a little autographed something, or just to say hi. In the meantime, happy reading!

Warmest regards,

Anne Eames

c/o Silhouette Desire
300 E. 42nd Street, 6th Floor
New York, NY 10018

One

The last place Jake Alley wanted to be on this hot, cloud-less Saturday evening was in a hot, humorless chapel, watching some fool surrender his freedom.

His bumper sticker didn't lie. He'd rather be sailing. Or at the very least, downtown Detroit at Tiger Stadium for the twi-night doubleheader. Anywhere other than this highfa-lutin Birmingham wedding would be an improvement.

But there he sat beside Aunt Helen, his shirt stuck to his back, wondering if dark blotches were beginning to show through his new khaki suit. Why had he let himself get roped into this? He didn't even know these people—Cath-erine something-or-other, the daughter of Aunt Helen's boss, and the supposedly handsome hunk she had snared. Poor sap.

The organist struck a loud chord. Jake stood along with the others, fanned his opened jacket against his soggy shirt and started calculating how much longer before he could be on his way. He'd drive Aunt Helen to the reception, grab a brew or two and sit with her through dinner as promised.

Sounded like at least three hours. Unless he could find her a ride...

Aunt Helen jabbed her elbow into his side and for a guilty second he thought she'd read his mind. She nodded her head toward the aisle. Behind him he heard the slow, rhythmic swishing of fabric skimming the surface of the white runner. The naturally rebellious part of him wanted to stare straight ahead and ignore convention, but with a resigned sigh he turned to the right and cast an aloof look up the aisle.

That's when he saw her. The bride drew closer, almost in slow motion, the surreal moment isolating each frame. He stared shamelessly at her long, black lashes blinking over humongous baby blues. Flawless skin radiated a healthy glow. Another step and her smile widened, exposing perfect white teeth. Then, two rows from him, her eyes met his. And in that brief instant, behind the perfect facade, he saw a hint of what was to come. A chill shot down his damp shirt. He tried to get another read, but she drifted past him.

Jake focused on her silky black hair swaying below a cloud of puffy white netting, wishing he knew what to make of her expression and wondering if anyone else had seen it. He didn't think it was wedding day jitters. He'd seen that look before. It was more like confusion bordering on panic—a feeling he could relate to this very moment.

Finally she reached the altar and turned to the tall man who had been waiting for her. Jake stiffened. It was as if someone were holding a photo in front of him asking *"What's wrong with this picture?"* Zooming in for a close-up he noticed the groom's possessive smile. Instantly Jake knew the answer. How he knew or why he cared, he wasn't certain. But in his gut he knew he was right. This man was not right for this woman. And somewhere deep inside the bride knew it, too.

Jake stood there, mouth agape, until he realized everyone else had sat down. Quickly he dropped into the pew, reality trying to worm its way back in but not succeeding. As the vows rolled on he replayed the scene over and over. That face, those eyes...

"I now pronounce you husband and wife." The minister's words pierced Jake's fog. He watched the pair smile at each other once again. "You may kiss the bride."

The organist pounded out another earsplitting refrain. A beat slower than the others Jake stood, this time refusing to look beyond his hands gripping the pew in front of him. When their turn came to exit he took Aunt Helen's elbow and shuffled out behind the excited crowd, feeling exhausted and emotionally spent.

A welcome July breeze greeted them as they walked down the church steps. Jake inhaled deeply and let out a long, hot breath, trying to find his old prehallucinatory self. He'd just about succeeded when a handful of something bounced off his chest and landed at his feet. He stared down at the tiny particles, expecting to find rice. Instead he saw bird seed.

"How appropriate!" he muttered under his breath. This whole scene was for the birds. He eyed the parking lot. His topless Jeep was sandwiched between two BMWs, reminding him this wasn't his world and he was wasting his time trying to figure it out. Suddenly eager to move on to the reception and a cold beer, he looked down at Aunt Helen. She was still watching the maudlin parade, dabbing her cheeks with a lace-edged hankie. Jake turned and walked a few steps, hoping Aunt Helen would get the hint, but she didn't budge. Patience exhausted he went back, hooked his arm in hers, and guided her to his Jeep.

Jake loosened his tie, fighting the urge to take it off and strangle his dear, sweet aunt. Thank God dinner was nearly over. How much longer could he pretend not to notice her meaningful glances—the ones that said "Why can't *you* find a wonderful bride?"

Wonderful bride. Now there's an oxymoron!

He rocked back in his chair and tried looking at the bright side. The chow had been better than usual and the drinks were free and plentiful. Best of all, he'd found a ride home for Aunt Helen. A few more polite minutes and he was out of here.

What on earth had come over him in that church to-night? he wondered, stealing another glimpse at Catherine what's-her-new-name, then quickly looking away. The tin-kling sound of silverware against glass meant Mr. Wrong would have his tongue halfway down her throat any second and he didn't want to watch.

Musicians caught his eye in the far corner and he shifted in his chair for a better view. He folded his arms against his chest. This wasn't at all like him. If anybody at a wedding deserved sympathy it was the poor, delusional groom, not the bride.

In spite of himself he looked back at the head table where the groom was kissing his way down the row of brides-maids, lingering especially long with the all-too-eager buxom blonde on the far end. Catherine seemed to be tak-ing it all in stride, smiling and sipping champagne. Tuxe-doed waiters hustled around obstructing his view, but each time the path cleared, his focus returned to her full lips, playing at the edge of the crystal flute.

Before long, not remembering asking or accepting, Jake found himself waltzing with Aunt Helen and wondering why in the hell he hadn't left yet. Two more beers and an hour later he was still asking that same question. He reminded himself his aunt had a ride home. Spotting her now half-way across the room, she seemed to be having the time of her life without his help. So what strange, masochistic im-pulse kept him in this place? It was too late to head down to Tiger Stadium. But that wasn't it. For some unknown rea-son he wanted to see this through to the end.

After awhile he lost track of the newlyweds and just went with the flow. Unattached males were in a minority so he found himself on the dance floor often, doing his basic clutch-and-shuffle, more than once with the tipsy blond bridesmaid who propped her Dolly Parton's on his chest for balance.

About eleven Jake sat one out, idly wondering where Dolly had gone but not really caring. He glanced around and spotted Catherine gliding gracefully across the dance floor, sans hubby. The temptation was stronger than ever to ask her for a dance. Why not? Every other guy in the room had had a whirl. Instead Jake slouched in his chair. He didn't trust himself. If he ever got her in his arms he'd tell her what a colossal mistake she was making—probably not what a bride wanted to hear on her wedding night. He continued to watch, unable to take his eyes off her as she approached the bandstand. The minister slowed her progress, but only momentarily. She snatched the paper he held in his hand, then moved purposefully to the microphone.

Slowly Catherine turned, the rosy glow in her cheeks all but gone. She motioned for the band to stop playing. "I want to thank you for coming." She paused and sucked in air. "You're all welcome to stay and enjoy yourselves for as long as you like . . . but I'm leaving."

As the crowd quieted, the nervous bride seemed to be stretching herself taller, mustering courage. Jake straightened in his chair, sensing something had run amok.

Then it hit him.

She'd said *I'm* leaving, not *we're*. Where was Studly? Quickly Jake scanned the room while the bride continued.

"If you brought a gift tonight, please take it home with you." There was a collective intake of air from the hushed crowd. Jake abandoned his search and stared at Catherine incredulously. Seeming determined to finish what she had started, she rushed on. "Those who sent something to the house, I'll see that your gifts are returned."

Jake followed her nervous glance to the table at the edge of the dance floor. Catherine's mother was clinging to her husband's arm like a lifeline and the older woman with a corsage sitting next to her began to weep.

The bride averted her gaze from her loved ones to an anonymous spot on the opposite wall. "The reason I'm leaving is that my *husband*—" she spat out the word "—of three hours and twenty minutes—" she made a dramatic show of consulting her watch "—is out in the parking lot with one of my bridesmaids . . . starting the honeymoon without me." On that note, with back straight and head high, she crumpled the paper in her hand and made for the nearest exit.

The door no sooner closed behind the bride when pandemonium reached ten on the Richter scale. While some openly cried and others expressed anger or shock, it was all Jake could do not to jump up and shout, "Bravo!"

It might have taken her awhile, but Catherine had finally discovered what he'd known from the first. The groom was a jerk. She deserved better.

A little voice inside added *Yeah, someone better—like yourself.* He drowned the nasty thought with a last swallow of beer and stood. He found Aunt Helen a few tables away, wide-eyed and excited, huddled with her ride home. Her hands were moving as fast as her lips and neither stopped when Jake approached. He bussed her cheek, then pushed his way through the confusion, feeling an urgency he couldn't explain. He didn't know what he was going to do or say but he had to find Catherine before anyone else did— this perfect and innocent creature—help her through this embarrassing ordeal, make her see the Fates had actually smiled on her.

It wasn't hard to spot all that white in the middle of the clear, dark night. She was pivoting wildly between two rows of parked cars, fists clenched. He expected to see flames shooting from her nostrils any second. He approached cautiously, wondering if she was looking for hubby, though he hadn't noticed any rocking vehicles, nor arms or legs protruding from unusual places. Then he understood the problem.

Where would a bride put car keys in a getup like that?

His role clearer now, he closed the space between them quickly, moving within a yard of her back before speaking. "Can I give you a ride somewhere?"

She spun around. "Who the hell are you?"

The sweet, innocent part of his fantasy launched itself to Pluto. This was clearly a woman capable of taking care of herself. Not to be deterred he held out his hand.

"Jake . . . Jake Alley." His hand hung out there. Naked. Exposed. She stared at it but didn't touch it. If she had he was certain it would blister. Slowly he slipped it into his pocket and tried to appear nonchalant. "I just thought under the circumstances you might need a lift.'' She was still breathing rapidly. ''Unless, of course, you have keys—'' she seemed to waiver for a moment ''—or you want to go back inside and find some.''

That did it. He had her now.

''I don't even know you.'' There was a slight pout on those great lips.

''That's okay...I don't know you, either.'' He turned and walked toward his Jeep. The sound of rustling material and clicking heels followed.

Jake opened his door and hopped in. He reached across the passenger seat and shoved open the opposite side. Catherine stood there glaring at him with a look that could send a pit bull whimpering into the corner. Then she turned, hiked up her big skirt, stepped backward onto the running board and jumped into the seat. She landed with a whoosh atop yards of satin, lace and what-all and Jake grinned.

She rotated in her seat and looked at him, catching his amused expression. He fully expected another angry outburst but, instead, she jammed the balled paper down the front of her dress, then ripped off her headpiece and tossed it in the back. Next she ruffled her hair, letting it fall loose around her face. Then she shot both arms straight up into the exposed night air and tilted her face to the moon, holding the pose for what seemed like the longest time.

Finally she dropped her arms into her lap and turned to Jake. ''Well? What are you waiting for? Let's go!''

Jake threw the gearshift in reverse and left a patch of rubber as he rounded the corner heading for Woodward Avenue and downtown Detroit. When he glanced at his passenger she was gripping the roll bar and eyeing him critically.

''Late for an appointment?'' she asked, not hiding her disapproval.

''New suit,'' he smirked. ''Didn't want blood all over it...duking it out with your husband.'' She rolled her eyes and faced forward, hair blowing out behind her, and he thought she looked more beautiful than when she'd walked down the aisle.

What in Sam Hill was he thinking? No matter how women came packaged, they were all basically the same. He eased up on the accelerator and reminded himself of previous experiences that bore out that sentiment. Images of Sally and her slick attorney were never far below the surface. He indulged his anger a few moments before braving another glimpse at Catherine.

When he finally looked, her head was lolled to one side, eyes closed. He wondered what kind of woman could sleep at a time like this? But then she spoke.

"He's not actually my husband."

"Really?" He pictured the pricey Townsend Hotel they'd just left. "Kinda expensive rehearsal, don't you think?"

She shot him an exasperated look. "You know what I mean..." Her voice trailed off as she turned her face to the far side. "...no consummation, no marriage."

Jake thought about the groom, Studly. He had consummated. Did that mean he was married but Catherine wasn't? He decided she probably wouldn't appreciate his humor so he bit his tongue and kept driving.

"Besides," she continued, sounding as if she were talking more to herself than to him. "We never completed the paperwork. The minister was trying to get us all together... that's when I went looking for..."

Jake glanced at her. She was staring intently at the dashboard. Then she turned to him.

"Do you suppose that means I'm not actually married?"

What did he look like—a lawyer? Heaven forbid. "Interesting question," he said, and wondered if she could be right. The light ahead turned red and he rolled to a stop.

A convertible full of teenage girls pulled alongside. Apparently spotting the mound of white surrounding his passenger, they started leaning on the horn. Jake pretended not to notice the kisses being blown in their direction and the clanking of keys against pop cans in the familiar symbolic gesture. Catherine slumped lower in her seat and groaned. For a crazy second he thought about planting a big, sloppy kiss on the bride and giving the girls the show they wanted. The light turned green and he stepped on the gas.

At the next crossing he turned right, pulled to an abrupt stop behind a vacant office building, and turned to her. "Isn't it time you got out of that dress?"

Her eyes widened. She turned away and jerked at the locked handle, ready to take flight.

Jake grabbed her arm and held tight. "Whoa . . . I didn't mean here." She tugged her arm free and rubbed it, still looking wary. "For God's sake, I'm not Jack the Ripper."

"Right," she said, and he saw her begin to relax, traces of a smile crinkling the corners of her eyes. "How stupid of me. It's *Jake* the Ripper, isn't it?"

In spite of himself he laughed and was rewarded with another glimpse of those perfect teeth. He studied her a moment, then slowly backed out onto the street.

Another time, another place, maybe . . .

He stopped at the corner. "Okay. Where to?"

"Back the way we came. About a half mile past is my maid-of-honor's house. I left a change of clothes there . . . and my suitcases for . . ."

For the first time he heard a quiver in her voice and he could almost feel her spirit float away with her unfinished words.

She didn't speak again until they neared their destination. "Next right. Second block, fourth house on the left," she said economically, then fell silent again.

He pulled up in front of a cozy Cape Cod and left the engine idling. What now? he wondered. "Nice meeting you? Have a nice life? Tough break, kid, better luck next time?" Suddenly he realized he didn't want to say goodbye and just drive off. For a fleeting second he let himself think she might be feeling the same way.

Hesitantly he draped an arm over the back of the seat. She turned and looked him straight in the eye. There was no evidence of tears, just an emptiness that seared right through him, stirring all those old he-man emotions. To hell with the new suit. He wanted to go back to the hotel and pound Studly to a bloody pulp.

Finally she said, "So . . . where you off to now?"

"Good question." He tipped his head back and admired the sky, waiting for an answer to come. One place was obvious. He grabbed onto it and exhaled loudly. "Oh, I guess I'll head over to Alley Cat." He hoped for some sign of recognition, but when he heard none he looked over. She was staring out the front window and he wasn't sure she'd heard him. "Ever go there?"

"Once."

"What did you think of the place?" He couldn't resist.

"I thought it was a perfect place for beauticians to meet wanna-be cowboys." She didn't even look at him, just opened her door, bunched up her dress and hopped out onto the perfectly manicured lawn. On the front steps she stopped and called over her shoulder. "Thanks for the ride, Jake."

Two

The key was in the corner of the window flower box where Becky always kept it. Catherine shook off a clump of dirt and inserted it into the lock. Once inside she shut the door behind her, leaned against it and heard the Jeep pull away. She filled her lungs with air, closed her eyes, and let out a long, slow breath.

No! She wouldn't think about it now. She had to keep moving. Impatiently tugging at her back zipper, she ran up the stairs. If she hurried maybe she could be out of here before anyone arrived. This would be the first place they'd look.

She found the new smoky blue silk pants and matching top laid out on the bedspread where she'd left them. A pair of white sandals waited at the foot of the bed, a small white leather purse beside them. The dress fell in a heap at her feet, the balled paper in the bodice tumbling loose. She scooped it up and shoved it in her purse, then kicked the dress aside. She continued kicking it as she finished tucking the top into the pants, the phone propped between her ear and shoulder.

A gravelly voice came over the line. "North Oakland Taxi."

"I'm a block north of Lincoln, east of Woodward. How fast can you get here?"

"Where ya goin'?"

She hadn't thought that far. Once she was in the cab she'd figure out the next step. For now she'd tell him anything. "Downtown Detroit."

Catherine gave the address, hung up and did a quick survey of the room. There were a couple of large suitcases by the door and a matching burgundy carryon. Ever since the first time her luggage had been lost on a buying trip three years ago, she'd always packed a change of clothes, swimsuit and all toiletries in her carryon. She eyed the suitcases a moment, remembering the hours of planning and shopping for just the right trousseau. Before the first tear could come she swallowed hard, flung the carryon over her shoulder and ran down the stairs.

For the first time she noticed the glow of a kitchen light and the note left on the counter. She looked out the front door. No sign of the cab yet. She debated a second, then headed for the note knowing what to expect.

The short message began "Dearest Cat and TJ—I'm so happy for both of you." She turned the single page facedown and picked up the pen left beside it.

"Becky, have to be alone for a while—sure you understand. Please call Mom and Dad—tell them I'm okay." A horn sounded out front and she scribbled a last line. "Tell them I'll call tomorrow. Love, Cat."

She flew down the walk and slid into the back of the cab. "Head south on Woodward. I'll let you know where in a minute."

Where could she go? Any decent hotel would do, but she wasn't in the mood for a quiet, empty room. What sounded better was a noisy room full of strangers—someplace where she could get a good, stiff drink and feel sorry for herself.

She opened her eyes and stared blindly at the passing blur of commercial buildings.

They were south of Twelve Mile Road before they caught a red light. The cabbie jerked to a stop, and she turned to see the flashing neon outline of a big cat just ahead.

Before she could think it through she heard herself say, "Let me out here."

He pulled to the curb, braking hard, then turned to face her. "Ya sure about this?"

The meter read eight and a quarter. She slapped a ten into his hand, got out and the cab sped off. She hesitated at the entrance to the bar. Given her current choices she slung open the heavy wooden door and strode in.

Just as she suspected, a country-western band was keeping two-steppers happy in the center of the room. On the perimeter, boot-stomping spectators kept time at beer-cluttered tables. If she didn't know better, she'd swear she was in Texas instead of Motown.

Slowly awakening from culture shock, she noted a few curious glances at her nondenim attire and shoulder-strap carryon. Self-conscience, she sauntered over to the bar on the right where a man she guessed to be in his late fifties sat in a wheelchair at the far end. There was an empty seat next to him. It appeared as safe of a place as any so she headed toward it.

"Excuse me," she said, raising her voice over a nearby speaker. "Is anyone sitting here?"

The man smiled up at her. "You, I hope."

The same words from anyone else might have sent her in the opposite direction, but this was the voice of a gentleman, one she sensed wanted a little company and nothing more. "Thank you." She pulled out the stool and sat down.

Her gaze drifted slowly over the crowd, looking for that one familiar face. *Why?* she asked herself. *Thought you wanted to be alone in a roomful of strangers?* She continued to look, taking her time, telling herself it was something to do. Anything was better than thinking about the disaster she'd just left behind.

She thought about Jake for a second, remembering his rugged good looks—sun-streaked sandy hair that swept back from windburned cheeks and hung a couple inches below his too-tight collar. She kept searching, smiling at a sudden thought. He must have felt as out of place at the Townsend Hotel in his suit as she felt here in her designer silk.

Catherine scanned the entire room twice, then gave up, feeling an unexpected disappointment. She swiveled around and rested her elbows on the padded rolled edge of the table-high bar. Curious about the unusual height, she looked to her right and noticed taller stools and the traditionally higher counter at the opposite end. Interesting. Was this end designed for the handicapped? she wondered. Or was the split level simply a decorator's idea to create a little interest. Whichever, she decided she liked it. She turned and smiled at the man in the wheelchair thinking he must like it, too. Then she let out a long sigh and glanced at her watch.

"Bartender!" The man shouted. "This pretty gal down here looks thirsty."

Catherine stole a quick peek at his chair and noticed there were no legs hanging from beneath the brown cardigan draped across his lap. She wondered what misfortune had scarred this poor man's life, but before she could think about it further, she saw a long, tanned arm slide a cocktail napkin in front of her.

"Well, well . . . slumming it tonight?"

Catherine looked up. "Jake!" She tried to hide the sudden rush of pleasure she felt at seeing him, but she wasn't sure she pulled it off. What was he doing behind the bar? His suit coat and tie were gone, shirtsleeves rolled to the elbow.

"What can I get you?" He was smiling coyly, probably relishing her discomfort, she thought, remembering her snobby remark about this place earlier. Determined to act as if this were any other night, that nothing unusual had happened, she forced a smile and answered his question.

"Something cold, wet and fattening. Surprise me." Jake flashed the okay sign and left. She stared after him a mo-

ment, then looked back to the man in the chair. His forehead was creased with curiosity.

"You know Jake?" he asked. "Don't remember seeing
you here before."

"I'm not what you'd call a regular." She swiveled toward him, still a little rattled at finding Jake behind the bar.
"We just sort of ran into each other earlier. He said he
might stop off here, but I didn't realize he had to work."

"He doesn't *have* to...he *wants* to."

She was about to ask what he meant when Jake returned.

"Here you go. Baileys on the rocks."

She took a generous taste, then rolled her tongue over her
lips. "Mmmm...good stuff." She stared into his dark eyes,
trying to read what was behind them. "How did you know
I'd like Baileys?"

"After you do this job for as many years as I have, you
know."

Jake wandered down to the other end of the bar and
Catherine's shoulders sagged. Great! She just got dumped
by a successful lawyer and she can't think of anyone she'd
rather be with than a career bartender. What sick twist of
fate brought her to these crossroads? Behind her, the fid-
dler went crazy while the female vocalist drawled her sad
lament. Catherine swirled her ice cubes and stared into the
milky brown liquid. Maybe coming here wasn't a good idea
after all.

"I thought Jake was at a wedding tonight," the man next
to her said.

Catherine kept her face forward and took another sip before answering. "He was. The party ended early." She
played with her straw, then bit the end of it. Maybe if she
went outside and let out a primal scream she'd feel better.

"Oh...then you were there, too, huh?"

A low chuckle emerged from the back of her throat. "Oh,
yeah...I was there." For the first time she tried to picture
Jake at the reception. She thought she remembered him
dancing near her once with a much older woman. She rotated her stool, deciding to take her mind off herself and fish

for a few details. "You seem to know a lot about Jake. Was that his mother with him at the wedding?"

The gray-haired man shook his head, the smile leaving his eyes. "Not likely!" After a slight lapse, he said, "You must be talking about his Aunt Helen."

Jake called down from the other end, "Ready for another Coke, Sarge?"

"Sure. And bring another for..." He looked at her and cocked an eyebrow.

"Catherine...Catherine Mason," she said and smiled.

"...bring another for Catherine here. She's dry."

"Thank you."

"You're welcome, Catherine." The fleeting distraction she'd seen in his eyes a moment earlier had vanished, the twinkle returned. "If I had a couple good legs, I'd ask you to dance. Used to be pretty good at the two-step. Can you two-step?"

She laughed. "Afraid not." She shook her head and laughed again at the mere idea. Then without much forethought she heard herself broach the delicate subject, embarrassed before she opened her mouth, but liberated by the accumulative effects of champagne and Baileys. "Sarge. Take it your name means you were in the army?" He nodded and she braved the next question. "Is that how...?" She looked down at his chair, then quickly back to his face and its pragmatic expression.

"Vietnam...another lifetime ago."

Jake reappeared with their drinks and for a brief moment she thought she saw a silent exchange between the two men. In a flash, Jake was busy with another customer, acting as though she didn't exist.

"So, Catherine, what do you do for a living?" Just like that, the subject of the war was over and the focus was back on her.

"I'm a buyer for Mason's." It was definitely time to leave.

"Buyer of clothes?" He was reassessing what she wore now.

She thought of the store, then co-worker Mary Beth—her last-minute substitute bridesmaid. She leaned her elbows on the bar. "That and other things."

"By the looks of it, I'd say you must do well at your job." He drank more Coke, then looked at the dance floor. Suddenly he waved his arm high in the air and motioned someone over, a look of recognition lighting his lined face. "Charlie! How you doin'?" he shouted over the guitar twang.

A good-looking cowboy about Jake's age sauntered over. Charlie patted Sarge on the back, then pumped his hand vigorously. "Doin' fine, Sarge. And you?"

"Couldn't be better." He looked at Catherine and extended his arm. "This here is Catherine. She's a friend of Jake's."

Before she could dispute the "friend of Jake's" line, Charlie grabbed her hand and shook it, a little more gently, and said howdy.

Sarge asked, "Got a date tonight, Charlie?"

"Nah. Just me and the boys."

"Then why don't you show Catherine here howda two-step. Jake's kinda busy and I'm not much fun."

Charlie took a step closer. With a smile wider than Texas, he extended his hand, palm up, and said, "Love to!"

"Oh, no!" Catherine shook her head and her hair flew side to side. "I couldn't, but thanks for the offer."

Charlie looked down at her left hand. "I see."

She followed his gaze, stopping at the new diamond-studded band sparkling on her third finger. The anger she'd been denying for more than an hour finally broke the surface. In one quick motion she jerked off the ring and shoved it in her pants pocket. When she looked up the men were exchanging a knowing look.

"It's...it's not what you think," she stammered. Neither of them looked convinced, but she wasn't about to explain. Instead she stood and pressed her fists to her thighs. It was time to move. One way or the other, she had to expel this mounting energy raging behind her ribs. Her gaze darted to the door, then to the bustling dance floor. This place might not be the answer, but it beat standing alone on Woodward Avenue after dark.

She looked back at Charlie with his thumbs hooked in his belt loops. He eyed her warily. She'd probably regret this in the morning, but what the hell. She could add it to the list. "Is that dance lesson still open?"

Jake watched the pair laughing and twirling around on the dance floor, a sense of déjà vu stabbing at his gut. They'd been at it now for over an hour. What was she trying to do? Rub it in his face? Tease and flaunt until he jumped over the bar, picked her up and carried her off kicking and screaming? He dried the same glass for the third time, then slammed it down on the counter.

Damn! What was the matter with him? He had no claim on this woman. Besides, she barely knew he was alive. She was simply here to forget her troubles like everyone else in the place. Under the circumstances how could he blame her?

The band took a break and Jake watched Catherine lead Charlie back to Sarge, who seemed to be having a vicarious good time. More than once since Catherine arrived, Jake thought about telling the old guy what happened to her tonight, but discretion won out.

He checked his watch: one-thirty. Time for last call. By the sway in Catherine's walk he hoped she didn't ask for another. Between dances she'd been slamming back Baileys as if they were milk shakes.

Jake walked over to Tom at the service bar. "Mind closing up alone?"

"No problem, Jake. Thanks for sticking around. When Tim called in sick I thought I'd be stuck here alone all night. I owe ya one, guy."

"I'll remember that." Jake smiled, patting Tom on the shoulder before heading back to the trio at the other end. Charlie was hanging over Catherine, practically drooling, and Sarge was laughing heartily at something she'd said.

Trying to appear uninterested, Jake strolled out from behind the bar. He stopped behind Charlie and spoke softly near his ear. "Too bad you have to leave now, my friend."

Charlie looked over his shoulder ready to protest when he met Jake's direct stare. Jake glanced in Catherine's direction, then quickly back to Charlie. Charlie got the message. Loud and clear.

"See ya around, Sarge, Catherine," Charlie said, his disappointment showing.

Catherine turned abruptly and looked up. For a moment Jake thought she might fall off the stool. "You can't go, Charlie. Who am I going to dance with?"

Jake stepped between them and took her hand as the band began its last short set. "Guess you'll have to settle for me." He gave her a not-too-gentle tug and she stumbled behind him onto the dance floor. When he spun around to face her he pulled her close and she landed hard against the length of him, but not without a giggle.

She snuggled her head against his shoulder and made a mewing noise into his chest. Her arm was draped loosely around his neck. It felt as though she might fall asleep any second. He tightened his grip, knowing he should take her home, but enjoying the feel of her far too much to leave.

It was hot under the dance floor lights, just as it had been hot in the church earlier, but a chill passed through him when he pictured her then...and now in his arms. What was it about this woman that made him feel so protective? He'd seen enough to know she could take care of herself. Still . . .

The slow dance ended and as much as he wanted another he stepped back. He caught her hand in his when it slid off his shoulder. Her eyes were closed and she was listing to port. Gently he turned her toward Sarge, slipping his arm around her shoulder and guiding her back to her stool. When they arrived, Catherine made no effort to move. With his arm still around her Jake shuffled his feet in front of Sarge, feeling like an adolescent on his first date. He cleared his throat.

"I'm going to take this young lady home. Need a ride?"

"Nope. Charlie's bringing his car around. Said he'd give me a lift." He waved Jake off with the back of his hand and a sly wink. Jake picked up Catherine's white purse and turned her toward the door. Halfway there Catherine stopped.

"Carryon...I brought a carryon...."

Jake looked over his shoulder and saw the burgundy bag under the stool. "Stay right here. I'll get it." Jake propped her against a wall and walked back.

Charlie had returned and was unlocking Sarge's wheelchair. He stopped and poked Jake in the side with an elbow. In a stage whisper, he said, "I do all the work. You get all the fun."

Another time, another woman, Jake might have let Charlie think what he wanted. "It's not how it looks, buddy. Someday I'll fill you in." With that, he returned to Catherine and slowly eased her outside and into his Jeep.

About a mile up the road she finally spoke. "Didn't we do this part already?"

He glanced at her quickly. Her eyes were closed, head tilted back, hair blowing helter-skelter.

Before he could comment, she said, "I like your Jeep." From the corner of his eye he could see her turn toward him. "And I like you too, Jake. You're a nice guy...you know that?"

He wanted to believe she meant it and would remember her words tomorrow, but he knew it was the booze talking now.

"Where we going?" she asked, not sounding as if she really cared.

"Toot's Diner. I need some chow and you need some coffee."

Another mile and he pulled into the restaurant parking lot, hopped out and ran to the other side before his passenger could fall on her face trying to maneuver on her own. She accepted his hand with a teasing smile and fell against him.

"Oops!" She giggled and righted herself.

When they slid into the booth nearest the door a minute later, Jake saw a waitress eyeing him. She came over with a pair of menus and shot him a judgmental look. Why is it all women assume the guy is some lech ready to pounce on some poor, helpless female? This female was hardly help-less. And by the looks of everything, not poor, either. He shoved the menus aside and ignored them along with the waitress's scowl.

"We'll have a couple orders of eggs, ham and toast. Make mine overeasy with rye." He looked at Catherine. Her eyes were at half-mast; she seemed dazed. "How do you want yours?"

"Scrambled. Whole wheat," she said in a monotone.

The waitress started to leave. Jake called after her. "And lots of coffee, please . . . soon." She looked back, her lips a hard, straight line. Jake winked and flashed a toothy smile.

Catherine didn't say a word. She slumped deeper in the booth, the back of her head pressed against the cushion, a cheek resting on her shoulder. Jake watched her doze, wondering if he should wake her and force some coffee down, or let her sleep. When the aroma of hot food and the noise of sliding plates didn't budge her, he decided he had to say something.

"Wake up, sleeping beauty. Chow time." He drank his coffee and watched her come around. She looked ghastly. Her complexion matched the pale green upholstery. He'd seen the signs often enough to know what was coming. Sure enough, she struggled to an upright position and moaned aloud, clasping her head with both hands. She took one whiff of the food, then slid quickly from the booth.

Jake pointed. "Down that hall, on the right." He watched her snake a path to the ladies' room and debated whether he should follow. Nah. There were some things a person pre-ferred doing in private.

Ten minutes later Jake was just about to send the wait-ress in after her when Catherine emerged. Her mascara was smudged, her face wet and pale, but she walked straighter than when she'd left. It'd been years since he'd pulled such a stunt, but he remembered the feeling all too well.

She avoided his eyes when she slid back into the booth and reached for her water. She took a sip, then looked at him sheepishly. "Do I look as bad as I feel?"

"Not quite." Jake dipped the corner of a napkin into his water glass. He leaned across and started wiping away the black from beneath her lashes. She inched forward, staring back at him with such a soulful look that he wanted to slide in beside her, crush her against him and never let her go. Now he wished he'd gone back and taught Studly a lesson he'd never forget. How could any man throw away a woman like this?

When he tossed the napkin aside, Catherine grasped his hand with both of hers. For the first time he saw a hint of moisture pooling above her lower lashes. He watched, certain tears would spill any second, but they didn't.

She raised her chin and blinked them back, then spoke in a barely audible whisper. "Thank you."

"You're welcome."

She picked up a piece of toast and started nibbling at it, testing the waters. When that worked she had some coffee and a little more toast, then more coffee. Eventually she looked at him and caught his smile. "What?" she asked.

"Nothing," he said.

"Come on. What were you thinking?" She smiled a weary smile, leaning heavily on her left elbow.

"I was thinking 'She's probably still drunk, but at least she's a wide-awake drunk.'"

"Very funny."

"You asked."

"So... where do we go now?"

He liked the sound of the word *we.* "I was just going to ask you that question."

She fell silent a moment, looking as if she hadn't the foggiest notion. "I don't want to go home, that's for sure." She pushed her plate aside, eggs untouched, and nursed her coffee. The waitress dropped the check on the table and scurried off. Catherine reached it first. Jake tugged at it but she wouldn't let go.

"No. I insist," she said, challenging him with an unexpected show of energy. She pulled it to her chest, then began rooting around inside her purse. A bulging envelope blocked her path. Annoyed, she slapped it on the table and continued foraging until she found some bills. She was about to return the envelope to her purse when she stopped, a look of inspiration spreading across her face. Then she tossed the opened envelope in front of Jake, encouraging him to read the contents with a wave of her hand.

"That's where we're going!" Seeming pleased with herself, she slid from the booth and headed for the cashier. Jake read enough to satisfy his curiosity, then scrambled to catch up with her. She'd already paid the tab and was on the way out the door. Without breaking stride she called over her shoulder, "What time is it?"

"Almost three-thirty."

"We have to be at the airport at five-thirty." She stopped alongside the Jeep and spun around, loosing her balance momentarily. Looking panicky, she studied his features. "Hair's a little lighter and longer, but it'll work." She breathed a sigh of relief and jumped into the passenger seat.

Caught up in her enthusiasm Jake hustled to the other side and slid in.

"Do you live close by?" she asked breathlessly.

"Yes, but..."

She turned and faced him squarely, folding her arms in a mix of impatience and determination. "Look, Jake," she started, looking angry. "It's too late to change the name on everything. TJ's birth certificate and photo ID are in the envelope. All you have to do is memorize his birth date and address. How difficult can that be?"

Nonplussed, Jake stared at her.

She relaxed her hands in her lap and smiled at him imploringly. "Well? Do you want to go to Jamaica with me or not?"

Jake turned the key in the ignition.

Three

_____

"Mommm..." Catherine rolled her eyes at Jake, who was leaning against the wall next to the airport pay phone, grinning. "Please stop crying. I'm okay. Really." She looked down at her feet, feeling guilty for her mother's pain.

"I know how humiliating it must have been for you and Daddy, but..." She wanted to say *It was no picnic for me, either,* but she let her mother prattle on, not wanting to say anything that would prolong the conversation. After listening to a long litany of who said what to whom following her hasty departure, she finally interrupted. "I need to speak with Daddy... yes, Mom. I love you, too."

Catherine extracted the wadded paper from her purse and began smoothing out the wrinkles until she heard her father's worried voice. She tolerated a few more platitudes, then heaved a sigh and asked her question. "I know this is a terrible imposition, but could you call your lawyer and ask him something for me?" Quickly she explained the unsigned marriage license in her hand and agreed to call him back in a couple of days for the answer.

"Thank you, Daddy."

He began again in what sounded like a long lecture and Catherine shot Jake another exasperated look.

"Sorry, Daddy, they're boarding my plane…have to run. We'll have a nice long talk when I get back." A moment later she hung up the phone and exhaled a loud sigh.

Jake hadn't moved. His arms were folded and he had that same silly grin plastered on his face.

"Now what's so funny?"

He pushed off the wall. "Nothing at all. This kind of thing happens to me all the time. How 'bout you?"

Catherine couldn't help but smile. "I guess this is a little bizarre," she said, picking up her carryon and walking toward the gate. "I wonder how many brides have gone on their honeymoon with someone besides the groom?"

Jake walked close behind her and whispered discreetly over her shoulder. "Probably the same number as men who went with brides that weren't their own."

Catherine swallowed a chuckle, suddenly feeling wicked and, much to her surprise, a little excited. Maybe this wasn't such a crazy idea after all, she mused. Besides, there was a good chance she wasn't anybody's "bride," that she was actually a free woman. As long as Jake remembered this was a platonic vacation, maybe Jamaica could be more than a convenient escape. Maybe it could actually be fun.

An hour and a half after takeoff Catherine picked at her second breakfast of the morning, still feeling queasy, when the practical side of her took over. Using the most businesslike tone she could muster, she began laying out the ground rules to her traveling companion. They'd come and go as they pleased without checking with each other, taking meals together as the mood moved them, but with no obligations. Strictly a business arrangement. No hanky-panky.

"There's a master bedroom and a parlor with a hide-a-bed." She nibbled at her dry toast and thought about offering Jake the bed, but reconsidered. After all, she'd paid for this whole trip, thanks to her offer to pay for everything by credit card and get reimbursed from TJ later. The least she could do for herself now was take the bed. Besides, as nice as Jake had been so far, he was still a man, and men were on her lower-than-slime list today.

When she fell silent Jake took the lead. "I'll use the hide-a-bed. You can have the bed." He'd polished off his eggs and sausage with ease. He wiped his mouth with a napkin and returned the no-nonsense look she'd been giving him for the last ten minutes. "I have no problem with your conditions, but I have one of my own."

She waited, curious what it might be.

"I insist on paying half of all expenses."

She opened her mouth to protest but thought better of it. Even a bartender had his pride. It wasn't her problem how he'd come up with the money. She held out her hand. "It's a deal."

Jake clasped it and shook it firmly just as the flight attendant retrieved their trays. He released his grip in time to salvage his coffee. "I'd like more when you get a chance." He smiled up at the pretty redhead whose eyes betrayed a more than passing interest. The woman lingered in the aisle making small talk.

Catherine felt a twinge of something resembling jealousy. Quickly she shook herself and found a paperback in her bag. Before she finished the first paragraph of her new Janet Dailey novel, the flight attendant was back refilling Jake's cup.

After she left, Catherine watched Jake from the corner of her eye. He slurped from his steaming cup, then reached for the *Wall Street Journal* tucked in the seat pocket in front of him. Catherine bit her top lip to keep from laughing. Who was he kidding? She'd bet her grandmother's pearls that he didn't know the difference between junk bonds and junk mail. This trip *was* going to be fun.

Three hours into the flight, when they ran into turbulence, Catherine's stomach lurched and any idea of fun vanished.

God! How she'd be glad when this ride was over. Motion sickness had never been a problem before. But then she'd never had so much alcohol before, either. Another thing she could thank TJ for—if she ever spoke to him again.

TJ. She'd refused to dwell on him since leaving the reception, but now her mind drifted in that direction, the book on her lap long forgotten. She leaned back in the seat and felt the cool air on her face, not ready to deal with the past, but unable to put it out of her head.

They'd grown up together, their families having been close since before they were born. It was natural for everyone to push them together. They were both intelligent, educated, ambitious and—probably too important to both families—well-heeled. Money would never have been an issue between them. They each brought their share to the table.

TJ's philandering was no secret to her. In high school and college she was the one he had told his secrets to, sparing no details of his outrageous behavior. But when their friendship had turned to romance, she thought all that had changed, that he would never cheat on her. Especially on their wedding night!

So, she asked herself, how did she really feel about all this? The first word that came to mind was *stupid*. TJ had made a fool of her, embarrassed her in such grand fashion that she wondered how she could ever face all those people who witnessed her humiliation. Of course, she reminded herself, they never would've known what he'd done if she hadn't stood there in front of God and everyone and told them. But she had to. She wanted everyone to know it was TJ's fault the marriage had ended before it began. She wanted him to pay the price for his inexcusable behavior. A slow smile spread across her lips. If only she could have seen what happened when he returned to the banquet room. There probably wasn't a soul there who had a kind word for him. Even his experience as a smooth-talking lawyer couldn't have bailed him out of that mess.

A half hour later Catherine was still picturing TJ and Mary Beth trying to cover their tracks, letting her imagination run wild, when she felt the plane touch down in Montego Bay. She looked to her right and saw Jake dozing, his seat upright and belt fastened. And for the first time she wondered what kind of man would drop everything and fly off this way. As if looking for a clue she studied his relaxed face. It was handsome in a rugged kind of way—tanned, with white squint lines at the corners of his eyes. His nose was a little large, but it seemed to fit his long, angular face. His sandy hair was a little long, too, brushing the collar of his blue chambray shirt. She let her gaze drift south to his jeans. Flat stomach, nice...

"See anything you like?"

Startled, Catherine shifted in her seat, feeling heat rush to her cheeks. She looked into his mocking brown eyes, then quickly away. "I was just looking at what you were wearing. I knew you changed clothes when you stopped by your place, but I didn't pay much attention at the time."

"Don't you mean you were out cold when I got back to the Jeep?"

She could feel his stare, but she refused to look him in the eye. "I was catching a little catnap, that's all," she insisted, thinking she sounded a tad too defensive.

"Right." The plane rolled to a stop and Jake stood into the aisle. He retrieved their bags from the overhead compartment, handing Catherine hers and positioning his duffel over one shoulder.

Catherine followed him down the portable steps, the hot wind billowing her pant legs, a length of hair blowing across her eyes. Before they reached the terminal she felt the moisture on her skin and the humidity curling the hair on her neck. They passed through immigration uneventfully and, having no baggage to claim, went directly to the row of shuttle buses.

The tags on their carryons identified their point of destination and a driver waved them in his direction.

"This is your lucky day," he said in his lilting Jamaican patois as they boarded. "You are my only two passengers this morning...so we con go right away." He settled into the driver's seat, then looked back at them. "You are Mr. and Mrs. Miller, am I correct?"

Catherine didn't want to see the expression on Jake's face. She despised being called *Mrs. Miller*. Today of all days. She could imagine how Jake felt about being called *Mr. Miller*.

"You have the right couple," she said to the friendly driver, forcing a smile.

Satisfied, he started the van and made his way around haggard-looking travelers and a maze of buses and other vehicles until finally he pulled onto the narrow two-lane road heading west for Negril, their home for the next seven days.

And seven nights.

Nearly two hours later, when they inched their way around a last stray cow and turned into the circular driveway, the thought of sharing a room with this virtual stranger became more of a reality. Catherine eyed the entrance to their resort. A large flower-engulfed ceramic sign spelled out its name.

Decadence II.

What kind of place was called Decadence II? she thought as she stepped from the van. And what happened to Decadence I? She shook her legs and stretched, glad to be on solid ground again, though still reticent about her surroundings.

She'd let TJ make all the arrangements once they'd agreed on Jamaica. All she'd done was pick up the tickets. Now she wished she'd been less involved with her job and paid more attention to this trip. She paused under the large, open archway, then followed Jake inside.

They went through the business of registration, tolerating the "Mr. and Mrs. Miller" routine one more time, then wandered down the tropical, plant-lined path to their room. Catherine noticed scantily clad guests roaming the grounds and was instantly relieved. At least they were clothed. This wasn't a nudist camp.

What started as a lark last night, felt more like a trip to the dentist chair by the time the porter deposited their bags inside the suite and left them alone, staring at the king-size bed. Her woozy stomach did another flip-flop. What on earth was she doing at a place like this with a man she barely knew? Maybe he really *was* Jake the Ripper. How did she know?

Catherine busied herself with her carryon, hoping to take her mind off the bed. It didn't take long to unpack since she only had a swimsuit, sandals, one shorts set and toiletries. On the walk to the room she remembered passing a couple of boutiques. She debated whether now was a good time to go shopping. Truthfully she'd rather take a nap, but not with this man lurking around. Restless, she grabbed her shorts, went into the bathroom and locked the door.

When she emerged a few minutes later, hair pulled back and feeling cooler, she looked toward the open door wall. Jake was standing in the same spot, thumbs hooked in his back jeans pockets, studying the scenery. She decided to see what was so enthralling and moved beyond him, out onto the shaded patio.

A gentle breeze stirred coconut palms, the sound reminding her at once that she was truly on vacation. There was nothing as peaceful and soothing to a midwesterner, she thought, as the sights and sounds of palm trees. She let them work their magic, lifting her cheeks to the warm rays that peeked through overhead branches. Smiling, she gazed down the sprawling, sandy beach to the majestic Caribbean beyond. Colorful sails of vivid red, blue, orange and yellow tilted gently with the wind on the blue-green horizon. A few small whitecaps tumbled lazily toward shore and she could feel the tension starting to ebb with each new wave. Maybe she was being silly to worry. This Jake person seemed harmless enough.

Her vision narrowed as she watched a swimmer emerge from the water. His tanned, oil-slick body was young and firm and...naked. She gasped and turned away quickly, feeling a rush of heat on her face when she passed Jake. She ignored his devilish grin and went back inside, willing to bet anything he wouldn't let the moment pass without some smart aleck remark. And she was right.

"What's the matter?" he asked. "Never seen one of those before?"

She wanted to say "One of what?" but she knew exactly what he meant and wouldn't dignify his question with an answer. Instead she turned and headed for the door, calling over her shoulder, "Have fun playing voyeur. I'm going shopping." She grabbed a key off the dresser and left the room.

A nude beach. Just what she needed. If TJ were here, she'd ring his selfish neck. She adjusted the shoulder strap on her purse and headed for the Logo Shop, determined not to let it get to her. When it was time for the beach, she'd wear her bikini and ignore the exhibitionists, that's all.

Jake watched Catherine stride down the path, her ponytail swinging behind her, and the uneasiness he felt last night returned. What was it about this woman that unnerved him so? He'd been with his share of beautiful women, so it wasn't just her good looks. There was something more. That damnable little voice inside kept saying crazy things such as *This is the one*. Whose voice was that, anyway? Certainly not Jake Alley's. He was far too cynical to believe in ... in what? Love at first sight? He harrumphed and turned away from the door wall.

Why on earth was he here? What had possessed him to take off with a woman he didn't even know? It wasn't his job to protect her. Still, someone had to. She was bound and determined to come down here. After what she'd been through, he couldn't let her take off to some faraway island by herself. Could he?

He pulled swim trunks out of his duffel and changed into them. It had been years since he'd had a real vacation and he'd certainly earned one, but the timing couldn't be worse—what with Sally and her pin-striped lawyer leaning on him.

No, damn it. He wouldn't let those vultures ruin a few days in the sun. The problem would just have to wait.

He turned and left the room. A good swim in the ocean would cool him off, in more ways than one.

A towel slung over his shoulder, he trotted barefoot down to the hot sand and found an empty chaise. One quick look around and he made his decision. He peeled off his trunks, walked several yards beyond the breakers and then dived into the tepid salt water, taking several long pulls before coming to the surface for air.

An hour later, Catherine flung her packages across the bed and kicked her sandals off, looking anxiously around the two rooms. He was nowhere in sight. Good. She shed her shorts and tank top and darted for the shower.

She rinsed quickly, toweled dry and returned to the bedroom, impatient for the feel of cool sheets against her warm skin. She removed her purchases from the bed thinking she'd put them away later, when suddenly the door opened behind her.

She swung around and glared at the familiar figure. "Next time, knock first," she snapped, tugging at her skimpy towel.

"Next time, dress in the bathroom." Jake sauntered in, also wrapped in a towel, and headed for the adjacent room, smiling broadly as he passed. That's when she noticed he held his swim trunks in his left hand. It only took a second to figure out what he'd been up to. She stared at the parlor door after it closed between them.

Who was this man? And what had she gotten herself into now?

From behind the door, he called out to her. "The bartender at the beach said orientation is poolside at six. I'm going to catch a few zees till then." When she didn't respond, he added, "You can let go of your towel now...I'll knock before I come out."

Catherine looked down at the towel and her clenched fist and wished she could punch him with it. He seemed to be enjoying her embarrassment way too much—first, her disastrous wedding, then a bout of vomiting, now her nakedness, save for this scrap of terry cloth. Not to mention her hair was a mess and not a stitch of makeup remained. She glanced in the bureau mirror and grimaced.

Wait a minute. Why did she care what she looked like? He was only Jake the wanna-be cowboy. Jake whom she would never see again once they returned to Detroit.

Yes, sir. When she got home, things were going to be different. No man, especially the likes of Jake Alley, was ever going to get between her and her goals.

She turned and frowned. What goals? Before Saturday night she thought she knew exactly where she was headed—married to a successful lawyer with political aspirations. How often she'd pictured herself at his side, fashionable, friendly and a dynamo at fund-raising. With TJ's intelligence and charisma and her genuine interest in people and their plights, his rise could have been meteoric. Her shoulders sagged. Now it all seemed frivolous. Even her job. Buying trips to Paris, London and New York may have sounded glamorous and looked good on her résumé, but in truth she hated it.

She eyed the connecting door, feeling frustrated and weary. Then she threw the towel to the floor, found a new knee-length T-shirt in one of the bags, pulled it over her head and jumped between the sheets. A little sleep and she'd feel much better. Then she'd start working on a plan for the future—one where her dreams and needs came first, not one where she was merely a fixture on some man's arm.

But as much as her body was ready for rest, her mind wasn't. Her lids were no sooner shut than she remembered TJ smiling down at her at the altar. TJ mouthing his lies of till death do us part. TJ with Mary Beth in the back seat of his Lincoln. How could he do such a thing? If he wasn't ready to settle down, why did he go through with the wedding? And Mary Beth. They weren't the closest of friends but they did work together well. She had seemed so eager to help when Catherine's cousin became pregnant and bowed out of the bridal party. If there hadn't been a substitution, would any of this have happened?

A lump rose in her throat and she swallowed hard. TJ wasn't worth her tears. Besides, who was she kidding? If it hadn't happened last night, it would have later—maybe after children. She couldn't wait to talk with her father and find out if she was really married to the jerk. She rolled over and punched the pillow and tried thinking of something else. Anything.

The first thing that came to mind was Alley Cat and a small chuckle released the tension in her throat. She thought of Sarge. Such a nice man. And Charlie...two-stepping, laughing. Had she actually had a good time at a place like that?

Then there was Jake. She felt her limbs start to mold to the mattress as she hummed a nameless country ballad. She was nestled against his chest, feeling light...and safe...and cared for...

Jake woke with a start not certain where he was. Through a slit in the drapes a palm branch swayed. Then he remembered. He lay there a moment and thought about the impulsive decision he'd made at the restaurant this morning. Yesterday at this time he didn't even know this woman named Catherine...Catherine...

He laughed aloud at his own folly. He didn't even know her last name. If it wasn't Miller, then what was it?

He threw his legs over the side of the hide-a-bed and arched his back. A week of this mattress and he'd be crawling to the beach. He'd have to check with the front desk and see about a room of his own, one with a real bed. He'd better call Alley Cat, too, and let them know he'd be gone all week.

He pushed off the bed and strolled to the window, parting the heavily lined drapes and letting the late-afternoon sun spill into the room. Regardless of how he ended up here he was long overdue for a vacation. And this was as good a place as any. Probably better than most he might have chosen. If he was going to spend the week watching over Catherine what's-her-name, the least he could do was relax and enjoy himself.

A schooner, anchored a few hundred yards out, caught his eye and he wished he was on it. Eager to get a closer look, he found his binoculars in the duffel, donned a pair of cutoffs and a Detroit Tigers tank top, then rapped softly on the connecting door. No answer. He put an ear to it and listened. Nothing. He knocked again louder. Finally, assuming she had gone out, he turned the handle and strode in.

Catherine was curled on her side, covers kicked to the foot of the bed, her long legs golden brown against the stark white sheet. Her face was scrubbed free of makeup, giving her an innocent, vulnerable look, a face no less appealing than the model-perfect one he'd first seen coming down the aisle. In fact, he thought he liked this one better. He was studying her long black lashes when they fluttered, then opened to the size of quarters. She sprang up, her shirt riding higher on her thighs. Jake couldn't help but look.

"What are you doing in here?" She scrambled to the foot of the bed and pulled the top sheet to her chest.

"I knocked and you didn't answer," Jake said, meeting her angry glare.

"I bet," she snapped back. "With what—the pad of your little finger?"

"Look, I'm going down to the beach." He glanced at his watch and stifled a smile. "Orientation is in half an hour. Maybe I'll see you there." He started for the door when she stopped him with another of her barbs.

"Be sure you get a good look."

At first he didn't catch on, but then he followed her gaze to the binoculars in his left hand and realized what she was thinking. He thought about offering an explanation, but he knew she was in no mood to accept it. "Oh, don't worry. I will." He winked at her and left the room.

All the way down to the beach he imagined her slamming things around the room, lumping all men in one ugly cesspool of angry words. It was just as well, he thought. Let her blow off a little steam. After what Studly had done to her, she was entitled. In the meantime, though, he'd give her wide berth.

As six o'clock grew near, empty chaise lounges around the pool grew scarce. Jake waited patiently for the show to begin, idly watching the tall, lean Jamaican reviewing his notes. The binoculars lay on the adjacent seat, saving it in case Catherine decided to show.

"Is this for me?"

Jake shielded his eyes with the side of his hand and looked up. He removed the binoculars and motioned for Catherine to sit just as the social director began.

For the next forty minutes, the fresh crop of mostly pale bodies listened to the long list of amenities—tennis, volleyball, snorkeling, windsurfing, sailing, horseback riding. There was a disco and a piano bar with Karaoke. Then there were special events, such as a toga party, a pajama party, a catamaran cruise and a fifties dance contest. Everything, including meals and cocktails, were included in the package. No tipping and no need to carry money—unless you wanted to pay for something at one of the five shops. Even then you could charge it to your room.

Before it was over, Jake wondered where he would go to relax after this so-called vacation. Finally the director said there was one more thing they needed to know. There were two beaches.

The nude. And the prude.

Out of the corner of his eye Jake saw Catherine fold her arms across her chest and heave a sigh, leaving no doubt where she stood on the subject.

Someone from the crowd asked, "Where exactly is the nude beach?"

The smiling Jamaican said, "You'll know when you get there," which Jake noticed brought a laugh from everyone except his companion.

Great, he thought and rolled his eyes. If there had to be just one finishing school graduate in this place, why did she have to be with him? He reminded himself she wasn't really *with* him. With a sigh he pushed out of his chair and offered her a hand.

"The dining room's open. Ready for dinner?" She stared at his outstretched arm a moment, looking as though she was weighing the possibility of contamination if she touched him, but then she gave in and honored him with her hand. Ignoring her mood, he bent her arm in the crook of his and pulled her closer as they strolled inside the main hall.

Dinner consisted of a variety of buffet tables, artistically presented with ice sculptures, animal-shaped breads and an abundance of tropical flowers. There was more than enough food to feed the troops. Jake guessed the size of the crowd at about four hundred or so. Guests sat at cloth-covered tables on three different levels surrounding a dance floor. On both sides of the raised bandstand were wide, wall-free spaces, allowing diners a panoramic view of the pool, beach and tropical gardens. Since there were no bugs, there was no need for doors or screens and everyone walked in and out freely throughout the evening. In spite of lively chatter from an inattentive audience, a local vocalist was singing her heart out on the bandstand as if hoping someone would notice she was the next Whitney Houston.

Jake took it all in, surprised he didn't miss the hustle and bustle of Detroit. He'd made the call home and covered things at work. Now, after polishing off a generous plate of standing rib roast and potato salad, he sat back and watched Catherine pick at her salad and nibble daintily on a bread stick. He couldn't believe he was still hungry. It had to be all the fresh air. The dessert table caught his eye.

"Want anything while I'm up?" Jake asked, pushing out his chair. Catherine wrinkled her nose and waved him on. When he returned with a raspberry-covered wedge of chocolate torte, he thought she showed a little more interest, but she averted her gaze and sipped demurely on her tea.

"Sure you don't want a bite?" Jake raised a forkful in her direction.

"Positive." She kept her eyes lowered and drank more tea. Jake realized she'd been sick earlier, but he wondered if the whole week was going to be this way. He didn't consider himself a conversationalist, but this was ridiculous. By the cold shoulder he was getting, you'd think he was the one who'd cheated on her. He turned his chair to get a better view of the singer and took another bite of torte, trying not to let her get to him.

After the third consecutive love song Catherine said, "I'm not really in the mood for this."

No kidding, Jake thought, feeling a little restless himself. When she stood to leave, so did he, making one more stab at bridging the ever-widening gap between them. "I was thinking about taking a stroll around, check out the place. Wanna come along?'' He tried to appear as if he couldn't care less whether she joined him, but in truth, he wished she would. She cocked her head, weighing the idea, then graced him with a small smile.

"Okay...for a while." She turned and led the way out. They passed the pool and made their way down a long, winding path. Jake watched her almost black hair. Combed free of its tie it swayed behind her with each long stride. Just as at the wedding he had an overwhelming desire to reach out and stroke it, to feel its silkiness between his fingers. Controlling himself, he looked beyond her.

The last rays of sunset mirrored the surface of the sea beckoning them to the water's edge. Without a word they removed their sandals and padded lazily across the wide stretch of smooth sand, foamy waves lapping at their toes.

Suddenly Catherine stopped. Jake took a few more steps then paused, waiting and watching. She gazed into the dusky sky, a gentle breeze brushing her hair away from her face. Her eyes closed and Jake wondered where she was. Was she thinking about that dreadful reception? Or had she dealt with it at all. They'd barely been apart since it happened and he'd yet to see her cry. He was about to broach the subject when she turned and walked on, kicking a breaking wave in front of her.

Jake hated chatterbox women, but he wished she'd say something. Anything. But she didn't. He followed her from the shore to the trail leading toward their room. When they reached the door he stepped ahead of her and used his key. She passed in front of him without making eye contact, then went to the far door wall and peered out.

Her back still to him, she spoke. "Why don't you use the bathroom first. I'll wait until you're settled in the other room."

Jake stared at her rounded shoulders a moment, not ready to call it a night, but not knowing what else to say or do. Slapping his hands on his thighs, he sighed and said, "Okay, fine," and headed for his duffel in the next room.

A few seconds later, armed with toothbrush and paste, he returned and went about his nightly ritual in record time. He paused at the connecting door when he'd finished. She still hadn't moved.

"Well . . . good night then," he said and shut the door behind him.

Four

The steady lapping of waves tugged Jake from a deep sleep. He lay with his eyes closed and remembered other mornings when similar sounds began his day, when the motion beneath him hinted at what kind of a sail he could expect when he came around. It'd been nearly five years since he'd lost *Cat's Meow* to his ex-wife, Sally.

He still missed his boat.

He stretched lazily, then wandered to the window and tugged the drapes open. He expected a serene strip of sand but was surprised at the number of early risers already staking out choice spots. He stood there a moment planning his day—shave, shower, breakfast, then down to the beach. Tough duty. His cutoffs were on the floor next to the bed where he'd left them last night. He pulled them on, found his shaving kit and went to the door. All was quiet on the other side, but remembering yesterday he knocked loudly and called out her name. "Catherine." Silence. Louder, he said, "Ready or not, here I come." When nothing came back, he inched the door open a crack and poked his head inside. The bed was empty.

He pushed the door open all the way and saw the deserted room. The bathroom door was ajar and all the lights were out. He stood in the middle of the room, smelling her perfume, and realized he was disappointed she'd gone somewhere without him.

"Now look, Alley," he lectured himself aloud, heading for the john, "a deal's a deal." They'd agreed to come and go as they pleased. Why did he care where she was anyway. He'd just go about his day as planned. If he ran into her, fine. If he didn't, that was okay, too.

But at breakfast a half hour later, he found himself looking for Catherine and was disappointed when he left without success. He knew he wouldn't find her at the nude beach, but that's where he headed, determined to stick to his original plan.

About a dozen yards ahead and to his right, he spotted the familiar thatched-roof hut. The sign across the front read Bare Bottom's Beach Bar, bringing a grin to his face. He wandered over to it, deciding to grab a towel and something cold to drink before settling in. The same bartender from yesterday was drying glasses, his shoulders keeping time to the reggae beat that blasted from the radio behind him.

As Jake grew closer, the man smiled. "How's it goin' today, mon?"

Jake shot him a thumbs-up sign. "Great, Bernard. How 'bout you?"

"Better and better," he said, letting his gaze drift to the new arrival approaching.

An attractive blonde leaned on the counter next to Jake and ordered a Bloody Mary. She was tall enough that the wooden ledge came just below the tan line where her top could have been—if she were wearing one. Jake watched Bernard mix the drink and kept his eyes forward. As uninhibited as he prided himself in being, this wasn't as easy as he thought. Besides, he still had his shorts on. Maybe she thought he was here to ogle.

"Can I get you something, mon?" Bernard was smiling from ear to ear, probably all too familiar with this scene.

"I'll take a Coke. I could use some more lead."

"No problem, mon." Bernard filled a plastic tumbler and handed it to Jake. When the blonde walked off, Bernard leaned closer and added, "Bet your bar not as much fun as mine."

Jake laughed. "Bet you're right." He drank half the soda and then ambled toward an empty seat.

Catherine adjusted the straps of her swimsuit, rubbing the marks they'd left on her shoulders. Finally she untied them and tucked them inside. The elastic under the top felt moist and itchy from perspiration. She rolled over on her stomach and her bottoms crept higher on her backside. She tugged each side down, accidentally dropping her book. She grumbled under her breath, thinking there was something to be said for nude sunbathing. After shaking the sand from the pages, she found her place and tried to read, but she couldn't concentrate. Finally she put the book back into her bag and stared idly at the sand.

A tiny sand crab came out of a hole near her head and she studied it curiously. It began playing with a shriveled berry dropped from a nearby tree. Catherine watched for the longest time, fascinated by its dexterous movements.

By the time it went back in its hole, she felt the tautness on the back of her legs and reached for her sunscreen. She squirted the white stuff on her calves and began rubbing them vigorously and thought about her day so far. She'd had breakfast, took a long stroll around the grounds and gave serious thought to her options for the future. Then she went to lunch, back to the room to change clothes, swam laps in the pool and even waded a few yards out into the ocean—all without a word to anyone. She dripped lotion on her arms and rubbed some more. This wasn't like her. She was usually a social person. Here she was in this tropical paradise with a chip on her shoulder, acting angry with the world for something one self-centered man had done to her.

She put the bottle back into her tote bag and settled on her back, hands locked behind her head. Someday, somehow, TJ and Mary Beth would get theirs. But right now, it seemed a waste to spoil this gorgeous place with a bad attitude. She struck a deal with herself. She'd allow herself a few minutes a day to think about that miserable night, but the rest of the time she'd work on her plan for the future and enjoy the present. It was time she started having some fun.

She closed her eyes and felt the hot sun on her skin, the strong rays massaging away the tension that had clung to her since she'd run out of the Townsend Hotel. Then suddenly she felt the heat on her face disappear. Not remembering a cloud in the sky, she opened her eyes and saw the reason for the shadow.

"Jake!" She sat up quickly, tugging at her top. He looked around for an empty seat but there wasn't one. When he started to sit in the sand next to her she gave him a hard shove and he landed on his side.

"Sorry," she said, chuckling. "You almost sat on my crab."

Jake righted himself and brushed the sand from his hands. "Excuse me?"

"My sand crab." She pointed to the perfectly round hole that looked as if someone stuck a pole in the sand at a forty-five-degree angle. "I've been watching him. He's kind of cute and I didn't want you to wreck his home."

Jake looked at her, the corners of his eyes crinkling. She thought he might laugh at her, but he didn't. Instead he crossed his legs, looked down at the hole and stared expectantly.

Catherine sat quietly, wishing her new friend out of hiding.

After a few minutes when nothing happened, Jake found a fresh berry and placed it near the hole. They watched and waited a little longer. Finally they were rewarded for their patience. Fragile chelas reached for the berry. Catherine watched in fascination. Two closely spaced black eyes held the only color that separated it from the sand. For a moment she wondered if she'd inadvertently stepped on any of its relatives. From now on she'd watch where she walked.

When the berry disappeared down the hole along with the crab, Jake looked up.

"You surprise me," he said.

"How's that?"

"I'd expect you to shrink away from such things."

"I don't know that I'd like it crawling up my leg, but I like watching it." Catherine smiled at his amused expression and found herself staring into his dark brown eyes a little longer than was comfortable. She averted her gaze back to the sand. "I guess I haven't been much fun so far." She expected some smart remark but none came.

He stood and wiped sand off his legs. "I don't know about you, but I've had enough sun for one day."

Catherine stood, pulled on her black gauzy cover-up and said, "Me too."

They walked along the shore toward the room in companionable silence, Catherine feeling more relaxed than she had since they'd arrived. Longer than that, now that she thought about it.

"It's none of my business," Jake started hesitantly, then pushed on. "But I was wondering if you called your father back."

"About the marriage license?"

"No." He rolled his eyes. "To ask what number sunscreen to use."

Catherine kicked foamy water at his legs. "Not yet, but I will. Thought I'd give him a little more time to find his lawyer."

"Lawyers!" It was Jake's turn to kick a wave.

Catherine watched his jaw clench and unclench and wondered what precipitated his angry scowl. But before she could ask, his expression changed and he glanced over at her.

"I have to say...you're taking this whole thing fairly well."

Catherine looked down at her feet and kept moving. He couldn't see or feel the lump in her chest she'd been trying to exorcise all day—which was just the way she wanted to keep it. Putting on a whimsical expression, she asked, "Do you suppose once I get past the anger I'll be able to see some humor in all this mess?" When Jake didn't answer she stole a quick peek at his face. He was scowling again, looking lost in troubles of his own. Had something similar happened to him? Something told her not to ask. Instead she continued with her train of thought.

She pictured herself in Jake's Jeep and how they must have looked cruising down Woodward Avenue.

They reached their room, and Jake unlocked the door. Catherine passed in front of him, biting back a smile. When she stopped and turned around, he was right behind her, a scant few inches away. "You've been very patient with me," she said, suddenly embarrassed under his close scrutiny. She felt her cheeks tingle and doubted it was sunburn. Her gaze dropped to his furry chest and she struggled to get out the next words. "Thank you."

He tilted her head up with his index finger and smiled. "No problem, mon."

She laughed and walked toward the bed, eager to put some space between them.

The room had been cleaned and the bed made, but two folded sheets rested atop the spread. Catherine picked them up. "Do you think housekeeping forgot these?"

"Don't you remember what they said about tonight? 'No sheet, no eat.'"

She stared incredulously at the thick white pile in her hands. "*These* are supposed to be togas?"

"If I remember correctly, you're in the fashion business."

"Not for long," she said under her breath before turning to face him.

Jake took a sheet from her and held it midair. "I bet you could work wonders with this thing if you put your mind to it." He cocked an eyebrow and gave her a challenging smile. "There's a contest for best couple, you know."

If she was serious about changing her attitude, now was the time to prove it. She threw her arms out in mock surrender and then let them drop. "Okay. I'll give it my best shot. Showers first, though." She motioned to the bathroom for Jake to go ahead.

"You go first," Jake said. "I'll just experiment with this thing till you're done."

When Catherine stepped out of the bathroom, towel tightly secured, she caught sight of his masterpiece and broke into hysterical laughter. The bulky white material had been tied like a giant diaper around his midsection. A long tail trailed out from behind.

When he stopped laughing at her reaction, he asked, "You don't like my creation?"

She spun him around and fought an impulse to tug on the tail. Afraid the whole thing might give way, and not sure what was under it, she put her hands on her hips and shook her head.

"Interesting…but not too Roman. Go take your shower and I'll think about it." He untied his sheet and threw it on the bed, revealing cutoffs underneath.

As soon as Catherine heard the shower, she found a pair of white panties and stepped into them before playing with her sheet. She knotted two ends together and slipped it over her head, being sure her top was covered before Jake reappeared. By the time he came out, she was twisting a long section into a rope and wrapping it around her waist. There was a slit up her right leg that stopped short of her underwear. He was eyeing her thigh suspiciously.

"Turn around."

She pirouetted, proud of her improvisation.

"Uh, uh, uh." He wagged a finger at her.

"What's wrong?"

"I see panty lines. There's going to be a toga cop at the door. Nothing but a sheet is law tonight."

She stared at his folded arms a moment, weighing the options. Then the solution came to her. She told him to get rid of the towel and put on shorts. After she was done costuming him, and they were both safely covered, they could slip out of their undergarments. Jake agreed.

Nearly an hour later, as they were about to leave the room, Catherine took one last look at their reflections in the mirror.

"Not bad, but something's missing." She snapped her fingers. "I know. Don't move." She raced outside and seconds later came back with sprigs of fern. Attaching a few to the knots at their shoulders, she stepped back and inspected the finished products.

"There. Now we're ready."

All through dinner Catherine made an effort to keep her knees locked together tightly. Other than that, she had to admit she was pretty comfortable in nothing but a sheet. She was feeling a little wicked, too. What would her mother say if she saw her at the dinner table dressed this way?

A waitress cleared the table and asked if they wanted an after-dinner drink. Catherine thought about a Baileys, but Saturday night's experience was too fresh.

"I'll have an Irish coffee, please."

"Make mine a Red Stripe," Jake said, and the young woman sauntered off.

The band had started and couples were making their way onto the dance floor. Catherine noticed the blonde at the next table who was studying Jake's profile for the umpteenth time. The V of her toga plunged to her waist. There were no tan lines above or below the ample, exposed cleavage. When she moved, Catherine noticed there was no bounce or even the slightest sag. Catherine wondered if Jake had met this woman at "his" beach, or if she was imagining the whole flirtation. After catching Mary Beth with TJ, she wondered if she'd ever trust another big-busted blonde. But then, in this case, what did it matter? Jake was not really with her. Still, the blonde didn't know that.

The next time their eyes met, Catherine tried deflating the woman's silicone with a dagger stare. The bust line stayed intact, but the woman shifted in her seat, turning her back to Jake. Catherine felt a smug satisfaction tug at the corners of her mouth just as Jake looked her way.

"Private joke?" he asked.

Catherine lifted her Irish coffee and took a sip, trying to swallow her smile, but instead she came up with a whipped cream mustache and started to giggle.

"Having a good time?" He smiled into his beer.

"Yes!" she said emphatically, somewhat surprised that it was true. "Yes, I am." She licked the rest of the cream off her upper lip and sat her mug down. When she looked back at Jake, he was still smiling, his eyes lingering on hers.

"Want to dance?" he asked casually.

She glanced at the dance floor, then back to his mouth. She liked his mouth. "Dance?"

"Yeah, you know...two people, together, moving their feet around, trying not to step on each other."

"Isn't that what we've been doing since we got here?"

Jake pointed the long neck of his bottle at her and smiled as if to say touché, then poured the rest of the beer into his glass.

"Well?" he asked without looking up.

Catherine checked that her sheet was secure, then stood. "Why not?" She led the way down the steps, hoping she looked more poised than she felt. Eating in this outfit was one thing. Dancing in it was another. Jake was a good six inches taller than she was. What would happen with all these folds and ties when she raised her arms? She found a square foot of unused floor space and turned to face Jake.

As if sensing her apprehension, he kept a respectable distance and held her hand low. She looked to the side, avoiding his eyes. Her left arm rested on his forearm, her fingertips grazing his firm biceps. She hadn't noticed how well developed his upper body was. That was a lie. She *tried* not to notice. Today at the beach, dressing him in his toga...

His skin was hot to the touch. There was a hint of pink over his already tanned skin. She looked at her own arm and saw the same color. That must be it, she told herself. The tropics. All that sun today. And the humidity is high. That's what she was feeling.

Another couple nudged their way onto the floor next to them. As soon as they did their first spin, the woman pushed into Catherine's back, crushing her against Jake. She felt her breasts flatten against his chest. His arm tightened around her waist. When he looked down at her, she knew her cheeks were scarlet.

"Are you okay?" he asked.

She couldn't meet his eyes. "Fine. Fine." She noticed he didn't loosen his grip. For some unexplainable reason, she had no desire to move away. When the side of his chin grazed her hair, she snuggled closer, her cheek against his chest. Before the dance was over, she thought she heard him moan. He pulled away from her slightly. Two layers of sheet were all that separated flesh from flesh. Still not looking him in the eye, she imagined the problem. Every fiber in her wanted to inch closer, to test her suspicions. But she kept her distance, glad when the music stopped and put an end to what surely would have been a mistake.

They turned side by side and applauded the band as the social director stepped up to the microphone.

"Our panel of judges—" he stretched his arm to include the staff behind him "—has made its decision." The crowd grew still.

The same woman Catherine remembered checking them in on Sunday, was now holding up two bottles of Appleton Rum.

"The winners are this lovely couple right here."

Catherine looked over her shoulder, sure he was gesturing to someone else.

The registration lady whispered something in the emcee's ear and he spoke into the mike again. "I'm told it's one of our newlywed couples, Mr. and Mrs. Miller."

Catherine stood stunned, unable to move.

"Come on up here, you two lovebirds."

The crowd was clapping, well-meaning hands nudging them closer to the stage.

Catherine felt Jake's hand on her hip, guiding her along. *Okay,* she told herself, *just go along with it. Take the rum, smile, and it will be over in a matter of seconds.* Jake winked at her as they claimed their prizes. If he could be a good sport about this, so could she.

Catherine forced a big smile, feeling the corners of her mouth twitching. The emcee fiddled with a couple of logo key chains, presenting them as if they were keepsakes to be cherished forever. His vociferous comments about their togas fell to the background when she heard the familiar sound of clanking silverware begin. She tried to ignore it, praying she was wrong and it would go away.

The noise grew louder, more insistent. Her jaw tightened. Still smiling, she spoke to Jake between clenched teeth. "Now what, *Mr. Miller?*"

He turned her toward him, one hand resting possessively on her left hip, a bottle of rum hard against her right. The symbolic clanking grew louder, along with a few shrill whistles.

"I guess we'll have to give them what they want, *Mrs. Miller.*"

He tried to look put out but it wasn't working as far as Catherine was concerned. She opened her mouth to object just as his lips came down on hers. The cheers escalated but she didn't hear a thing except the beating of her heart, pounding like a mallet against her chest.

Jake's arms encircled her back and hers moved easily around him. He eased his lips away gently and then returned them, softer, moister, giving. When he finally stepped back, she met his steady gaze and felt the blood rush up her neck.

"Ahh, isn't that sweet . . ." the emcee cooed, "a blushing bride."

Someone from the crowd yelled, "Don't see that much anymore," and the laughter swelled.

Embarrassed, Catherine lowered her eyes. When she looked up, she expected to see a smirk on Jake's face. But there wasn't a hint of a smile, which only made her more nervous.

The band started playing again and Catherine started for the table, bottle of rum clutched to her chest. Jake caught her free hand and stopped her.

"Let's go for a walk."

She turned to face him. His eyes were dark and unreadable. She didn't answer, but held tight to his hand, feeling its warmth trickle through her.

He turned and led them out, past the pool, down the walk and over the cool sand, not slowing until they reached the water's edge. When he dropped her hand to remove his shoes, she followed suit, instantly missing his touch, hoping he would take her hand again as they strolled along the shore. But he didn't.

She walked close to his side, sandals and rum in her outside hand, her inside fingers dangling free and close to his, wanting desperately to reestablish contact. Holding hands— it was such a simple thing, she thought. She had done it often enough with TJ. But it felt different with Jake. Why was that? It was as though a current ran through him, out his fingertips and through her veins. Just as when they'd kissed, it awakened every nerve ending . . .

"Penny for your thoughts." Jake spoke softly, startling her nonetheless.

She kept her face forward, thankful for the dark, hoping he couldn't see her cheeks in the moonlight. "Just enjoying the scenery," she said. It was partially true.

"About what happened back there," he began.

Had he felt it, too? That unexpected jolt. She inhaled a mouthful of salty air and let it out slowly, her sigh lost on a breaking wave.

"I'm sorry," he continued. "It won't happen again." He kicked a stone and sent it skittering along in front of them.

Catherine watched it, feeling kicked herself, but not letting on. She'd been so certain she'd seen something in his eyes when they'd kissed. Now she couldn't think of a single response that wouldn't leave her feeling like a hypocrite, so she said nothing and walked back up the trail to their room.

Once inside she moved directly to the door wall, sensing his awkwardness as much as her own. She heard him deposit his bottle of rum and key chain on the dresser behind her.

"Good night, Catherine."

She waited a moment, but nothing more came. "Good night, Jake." She heard the door shut between them.

She stared out at the sea awhile longer, hoping he would return. When he didn't, a single tear trailed down her cheek. And then another. Until finally she dislodged the lump in her chest. Her shoulders heaved, but she silenced the sobs, not wanting Jake to hear.

She let the tears run their course, then dried her face with the hem of her toga. Jake was simply a port in the storm, someone to ease the pain of losing TJ, that's all.

Pain? What pain? Embarrassment, yes, but heartbreak? She shook her head and sat heavily on the edge of the bed. No. She wasn't heartbroken. Why was that? And why did she suddenly feel close to this man she barely knew?

Catherine lay back on the bed and closed her eyes. She had to get control of her emotions. It was natural to be upset, she told herself. Even confused and vulnerable.

But attracted to another man already?

Not possible.

Five

Tuesday morning, Jake pushed off the sagging mattress and swore. Why hadn't he asked for a new room with a decent bed as he'd planned the first day? He thought about the kindly registration lady handing *Mr. Miller* the rum last night and swore again. How would he explain needing another room after his display on stage? A lover's quarrel?

He found his swim trunks and pulled them on, feeling a sudden need for fresh air. This time when he knocked, Catherine answered.

"Come on in."

When he opened the door, she was pulling a brush through her hair and kept her eyes on the bureau mirror.

"I'm done in the bathroom if you want to use it," she said, not looking at him.

"Think I'll go for a quick swim first."

She bent at the waist, threw her hair forward and brushed some more. "I'm going for a walk before breakfast," she said upside down. "Want to meet me in the dining room?"

She didn't sound at all angry or distant. After last night, he thought . . . What did he think?

She flipped her hair back and looked at him evenly. "Well?"

She was smiling. Go figure. "Sure. See you there in about forty minutes."

"Great!"

Jake closed his mouth and left the room. He changed his mind about the beach and headed for the pool. A dozen laps might clear his head.

Women! Would he ever understand them?

Twenty minutes later, chest heaving, he pulled himself up on the edge of the pool. Gulping in air, he tried to make sense of the long-legged brunette who was wreaking havoc with his well-ordered life. Ever since he saw her walking down that aisle four days ago, he didn't recognize this new Jake Alley. He held his hands out in front of him for confirmation that he still occupied the same body. Everything looked the same. But he didn't feel the same and that bothered him. The last time he lost control of his emotions, it cost him dearly.

He stood abruptly and grabbed a clean towel off the corner table. If thirty-two years of living had taught him nothing else, it taught him women couldn't be trusted. Especially beautiful women. And damn, Catherine was that.

When he entered the dining area a short time later, he spotted Catherine sitting in the center of the room, sipping coffee and staring out at the sea. He stopped and watched her. She was truly beautiful, in a classic sort of way. Long neck, high cheekbones. Not once had he seen her acting as though she knew what effect she had on men. Yet how could she not?

She turned his way and waved, flashing him those perfect teeth and he felt his control slip another notch. He ambled over to the table, trying to appear aloof, not sure if he'd succeeded.

They ate and made small talk and all the time Jake felt his frustration mounting to the point where he wanted to pound his fist on the table. But he held it in check. He didn't think she was trying to manipulate him, but that's exactly how he felt. She certainly couldn't be interested in him. After all, she just married someone else last week. Legal or not, she must have cared about the jerk—impossible as that seemed.

Jake finished his coffee and looked outside. The sky was slightly overcast. A few gray clouds hinted at a possible shower later on. A couple of sailboats had picked up wind and were moving along at a good clip. He slapped his knees, drawing a curious glance from Catherine.

That's what he'd do. Go sailing. At least out on the water, the sheet tugging in his hand, the boat responding, he could feel in control again. Eager to get on with his plan, he told Catherine his intentions.

"Sounds like fun."

She was eyeing him with a cute, imploring look. Before he could stop himself, he asked, "Want to come along?"

Excitement danced in those gorgeous blue eyes. "I'd love to," she said.

He was afraid she'd say that.

"You can put the centerboard in now." When he didn't hear anything, he glanced at her. She looked embarrassed and averted her eyes.

"It would be a lot easier if you helped," he snapped, not meaning to sound so gruff. She glanced around helplessly and he finally understood the problem.

"See that wood thing by your feet?"

Catherine nodded.

"Put it in that slot next to your legs." She did as she was told, losing her balance.

"Don't tell me you've never been sailing before?" he asked, enjoying the extra edge it gave him.

"You needn't sound so superior about it." She lifted her chin. "I'm sure I've done a few things you haven't," she added haughtily.

Right. Like go to the opera.

What was the matter with him? He was acting like a jerk while she was doing better than probably anyone else in her shoes.

As they tacked back and forth, bathers on shore grew smaller and smaller. Though barely a word had been spoken, Catherine seemed pleased with herself.

Jake watched as she tilted her face to the sun and closed her eyes. Her hair whipped across her face and she swung her head into the wind to clear it away before she broke the comfortable silence.

"You know, I've been doing a lot of thinking since we arrived on this island."

Jake watched and waited as she seemed to be organizing her thoughts. Her hands were relaxed atop her parted thighs. A towel, tucked into the strap of her safety belt, hung between her legs. Always the lady, he thought.

"Maybe last Saturday was meant to be my wake-up call."

There had to be an easier way, he thought, but kept his mouth shut and listened.

"I don't mean just finding out what kind of man TJ is." She glanced at him quickly, then turned her face back to the wind. "But finding out how shallow my own existence has been."

Oh, brother. Analysis time. Was he supposed to play shrink now? Whatever she expected, he knew enough about women not to agree with her. He remained silent, glad she wasn't looking his way.

"So I've decided to quit my job when we get back."

Now she looked at him. His mouth was open and he stared at her in disbelief. Apparently his reaction was unimportant, because she didn't falter.

"I've been thinking about all kinds of interesting things I could do that would feel far more rewarding than the fashion business."

There was a glint of excitement in her eyes he hadn't seen before, but still, he couldn't keep from commenting any longer. "I know TJ hurt you—badly—but quitting your job? Don't you think you might be overreacting a little?" He saw the fire in her eyes before she turned away.

"No, I don't." She raised her chin a notch. "And another thing I've decided, I don't need a man in my life." She glared at him. "Certainly not for a long time. And certainly not now—to tell me what I should or shouldn't think or do.''

She was right. He'd been out of line to voice his opinion. Besides, he knew just how she felt. He didn't need a woman in his life for the same reasons. And more. Still, it wasn't his nature to apologize over something so trivial, so he let the obvious affront pass.

Before long she closed her eyes and her jaw muscles relaxed. In spite of her outburst and inexperience with sailing, she seemed to be enjoying herself. Eventually, when the sun went behind a cluster of clouds, they headed back.

It was another forty minutes before they neared shore. The sun was beginning to peek out from behind a last remaining cloud. The temperature was still in the eighties.

Jake felt more alive than he had in years. The smell of salt filled his nostrils as he inhaled deeply and let out a satisfied sigh. From his perch aft, he had an excellent view of Catherine's bikini-clad body. Under other circumstances, he might have let out a wolf whistle in fun, but he'd probably get a centerboard upside his head if he said or did one wrong thing. So he smiled and enjoyed the scenery.

Jake pulled the boat ashore, taking his time. He wished he could go back to the room but he guessed that was where Catherine would be headed and he figured they could use a break. He'd avoid her for a while. Stop and see Bernard at the bar. Maybe find a shady spot and take a nap.

Yep. The more distance he kept between himself and Lady Catherine today, the better.

At seven-thirty that night, Catherine stood outside their room, ear pressed to the door, listening for telltale signs of Jake on the other side. She'd managed to avoid him all day, a day that had been productive and filled with good things, in spite of its shaky start.

First she'd found a quiet spot and made progress on her goals. Later she'd gone horseback riding off the grounds and worked up the courage to call her father, who had given her the good news she'd wanted to hear about her nonexistent marriage.

Satisfied that Jake wasn't in the room, Catherine used her key and walked in. As easy as it had been avoiding him during the day, tonight would be trickier. He was bound to be in the dining room and she couldn't wait to eat any longer. Her stomach had been growling for over an hour.

After a quick shower and change of clothes, she wandered down the path to the main hall, the sounds of reggae music growing louder as she approached the open space. She liked the idea of no walls on two sides. It gave her the opportunity to slip in anywhere, unnoticed. With hundreds of diners, she wondered if it was possible for him not to notice her. She spotted an empty table on the perimeter and moved toward it quickly.

It took less than a minute to find him. He was two levels down, near the dance floor, applauding the band. His back was to the buffet tables and she decided to take advantage of it.

Forty minutes later, finishing the last bite of her cheesecake, he still hadn't looked her way. She should leave now and go back to the room. She could read in bed until she heard him, then switch off the light and fake sleep. It sounded like a good idea, she told herself, as she pushed from the table.

Until she spotted the siliconed blonde stooping over Jake's table.

Catherine stared, her mind saying *leave,* but her body unable to move. She'd been right after all. That woman had been coming on to Jake last night. What nerve! As far as everyone knew, Jake was a married man on his honeymoon. What colossal gall! Catherine felt her chest rise and fall, fighting an urge to march right down there and smack the bimbo a good one.

Then Jake stood up and followed the bimbo onto the dance floor.

When the woman spun around and pressed her rock-hard melons against Jake's chest, Catherine stopped twisting the napkin in her hand and threw it on the table. With one last lingering look, she left the hall and strode down the path to the beach, kicking anything she could find in the sand as she went along.

The reggae followed her down to the water, its slow repetitive beat stirring something primitive, leaving her confused and gasping for air. She dropped onto a lounge chair and closed her eyes. All she could see was Jake and that woman.

She massaged her temples and forced herself to think rationally. Why shouldn't he dance with someone else? He wasn't her husband. He wasn't her date. For God's sake, he wasn't even her friend. Then why was it bothering her so? If she didn't know better, she'd think she was jealous.

Slowly she opened her eyes and stared out over the moonlit sea, the steel drums behind her evoking something sad and lonely now. A warm breeze lifted her hair from her moist neck and shoulders, sending goose bumps skittering along the surface of her skin.

She thought about this afternoon's conversation with her father. At the time she had felt elated that she wasn't Mrs. Miller, and never would be. Now, alone on the beach, she felt empty and adrift.

Again, images of TJ in his tuxedo mouthing meaningless vows, floated in and out. This time she let them linger, testing the feel of each new vision, putting a name to each new wave. All kinds of emotions swirled around—anger, betrayal, embarrassment, shock. But as she suspected last night, one telltale feeling was missing—the acute pain of losing someone she loved.

Angry with her own foolish behavior, she sprang to her feet and strode back to the room. She avoided the beach and cut through a path between buildings, lecturing herself with each long stride. Her whole life was ahead of her. That's what she needed to concentrate on. It was time to forget TJ and focus on a new plan. Something she could feel proud of, useful.

She let herself into the empty room and got ready for bed, determined to remain calm and unemotional, though every inch of her wanted to throw something and scream. She ignored the book on the nightstand, turned off the light beside the bed and pulled the sheet to her chin, all the time trying to think of the future and what she might do.

Restless, she rolled to her side. When she got home, she'd apologize to her parents for her temporary insanity. But for now, she was tired of trying to absolve her own guilt. She closed her eyes but they wouldn't stay shut. There were other things she had to sort out. She liked order in her life and since Saturday, she'd seen and felt nothing that resembled order.

The room had cooled and she reached for the blanket at the foot of the bed and then exhaled a heavy sigh. "Okay, Catherine Mason, what else is churning around in there?" she asked aloud, tucking the cover beneath her arms.

Something besides her disastrous wedding troubled her and she knew what it was. It was the thought of abandoning the business Granddad founded more than a half century ago. It seemed tonight was a night for guilt and self-incrimination.

Catherine could still see the sparkle in Granddad's eyes when she was only sixteen and asked him if she could work at the store part-time. You'd think she'd given him the greatest gift, especially since neither of her parents had worked the business and outsiders would manage once he stepped down.

What would he say now that she was planning to leave Mason's? A tear slid down the side of her face and she turned into the pillow to blot it away. If only he were here to discuss her decision, not to mention what happened at the reception. She wondered if he would have been as shocked as everyone else. Something told her he wouldn't; he was such a wise man. Granddad knew her almost-husband as well as anyone. TJ's father was the family's attorney and TJ worked in his father's firm, which also meant he knew all about Granddad's will.

Suddenly the thought struck her. Had she simply stayed with TJ because he had money of his own and knew the size of the estate she was about to inherit this fall? In a way it made sense. It was certainly easier than questioning the motives of any new suitor. Realistically what normal working-class man wouldn't be overwhelmed once he knew just how much...

She heard the key in the door and quickly rolled to the opposite side before Jake tiptoed in. She lay motionless, inhaling and exhaling long and slow.

When she heard the bathroom door close and the water start to run, she let out a loud sigh and looked over her shoulder at the digital clock. It was only ten-fifteen. Hmmm. Wonder what happened to Bimbo? Catherine lay on her back smiling and wondering why his early return even mattered, when she heard the latch. Quickly she rolled back and resumed her deep breathing until the door to the parlor closed softly between them.

She didn't move for the longest time, listening to every little sound in the next room, picturing his movements—the squeak of springs when he opened the hide-a-bed, the thud when its end legs hit the floor, his belt buckle and zipper, another squeak when he sat down on the mattress. She heard shoes dropping to the floor, pants with change still in the pocket sliding down his legs, the rustling of the sheet, punching of the pillow. Then silence.

She rolled on her back trying not to make a sound. She listened for some time but didn't hear a hint of sleep on the other side. Finally her own limbs sank further into the mattress and she felt herself slip away, mildly aware that her last thought was of Jake...wondering what he would do or say if he knew what TJ knew—how wealthy a woman she was about to become.

After a fitful sleep, Catherine awoke early Wednesday morning and left before Jake could knock on the door. With careful planning, it wasn't until dinner the next night that they bumped into each other. Literally.

Catherine balanced a bread stick on the edge of her salad plate and turned right into Jake's chest. She grabbed the teetering bread and stared straight ahead at the light brown curly hair jutting out from above the blue tank top. He smelled of coconut tanning oil. She stepped to the right. He moved left. She stepped left and he blocked her path again, this time speaking.

"Aren't you tired of this cat-and-mouse thing?"

In truth she was. But she'd never admit it. Finally she looked up. One corner of his lip curled higher than the other in that devilish grin she had come to expect. And like. It reminded her of Sam Elliott's smile in a TV miniseries she'd seen. She took a bite of bread stick and crunched loudly, stalling for time, hoping something clever would come as she held his steady gaze. This whole thing was silly and she knew it. But where did she begin? Unable to look him in the eye another second, she glanced away, spotting the menacing blonde from Tuesday, her nonbouncing, silicone enhancements moving pointedly in their direction.

Jake looked over his shoulder, then turned back abruptly.

"Damn! Can't that woman take a hint?" His exasperation sounded sincere. "Do me a favor. Have dinner with me," he whispered as the woman grew closer.

Catherine took his outside arm and turned him toward the bandstand without a second's thought. "Why don't we sit near the dance floor tonight, *sweetheart*," she said clearly so the woman could hear.

"Sounds great, *honey*." Jake said even louder.

He winked at Catherine who kept moving, pretending not to see the motivation for their little charade as the woman sashayed past with her collagen pout.

As soon as they set their plates on the table, they looked at each other and began to laugh. The ice had been broken.

Conversation flowed freely all through dinner, each sharing the excitement of the other as stories of the last day and a half tumbled out. Catherine even told Jake that the wedding was null and void, hoping for a reaction but seeing none. She decided he was either a very good actor or he didn't care one way or the other.

Eventually, she learned that while she'd been horseback riding, Jake had gone parasailing. Over dessert, she listened intently to every detail of his adventure, wishing she'd seen it. *If I hadn't been trying to avoid him,* she was thinking, just at Jake threw out his zinger.

"So when you goin' to the nude beach?" he asked.

"*Moi?*" Catherine tried to act surprised, but in fact she'd wondered how long it would take him to get around to the subject.

"Come on, don't tell me you never went skinny-dippin'?" He turned his head to the side, hiking one corner of his mouth in that devilish Sam Elliott way.

She forced her thoughts back to his question. Somehow, swimming in the buff in your own backyard pool wasn't quite the same. Nonetheless, she couldn't hide her smile.

"I knew it!" Jake slapped the table. "You're not as prudish as you pretend."

He was laughing now and she felt her back straighten. "I never considered myself a prude." She hadn't meant to sound so defensive, but she knew she had. "I'm just not an exhibitionist, that's all," she said more evenly.

"It's not like that down there."

She arched an eyebrow.

"Really," he insisted. "It isn't. Nobody's parading around or flaunting. It's just that it feels good to swim without a suit…or to lie in the sun and feel the air graze over your skin."

She had to admit, it did sound inviting. If the beach were empty.

As if reading her mind, he said, "You'll never see those people again. You don't know a soul down there, so what do you care if they see a little flesh?"

"That's not completely true."

"What do you mean?"

"I know you." *Aha!* She had him there.

"Do you mean to say, if I wasn't there you would do it?"

"I mean to say it's no big deal to take a little swim without your suit if you're surrounded by total strangers." Why had she said that? That wasn't at all how she felt. He'd done it again—goaded her into proving she wasn't the sheltered and uptight little princess he'd insisted she was from day one.

Regardless, she wasn't going to back down now. She squared her shoulders and lifted her chin. "You're on."

Deep dimples formed on either side of his wide smile.

When he continued eyeing her over the rim of his water glass, she thought maybe this had been merely a verbal game. Since she hadn't backed down, maybe she'd taken the wind out of his sails and the challenge was over. She decided to grab the sudden silence and run.

"Well—" she stretched her arms out and stifled a yawn "—I think I'm going to call it a night. All this fresh air makes me sleepy. It's been a nice evening, Jake." She pushed out from the table and started to walk away.

"Wait. I'll come with you."

She sighed and waited until he came alongside.

They left the dining room and strolled through the courtyard and past the duty-free shop, a loud chorus of crickets competing with the singer they left behind.

Eventually Jake picked up the conversation. "I think I have it figured out."

So much for the verbal game. Now how was she going to get out of this mess? She could always say she did it, but not. If he wasn't there when she went to the beach, how would he know whether she followed through?

"That black cover-up thing you had on the other day...it wasn't see-through."

She shot him a critical glare.

"Ah, come on. A guy can look, can't he?"

She rolled her eyes and kept walking.

"If you wore that down to the nude beach with nothing under it..."

She walked a little faster.

"I promise I'd wait in the room awhile. Then I could go down and see your cover-up on a chair and you in the water. That would be proof enough."

She used her own key and let them in. "Proof of what?" As if she didn't know.

"That you're not all talk."

She dropped the key on the dresser and turned to face him, sensing she had lost this round, but not ready to concede.

"How do I know you won't cheat and come down before I'm in the water?"

He chuckled and drew an *X* over his tank top. "Cross my heart."

And hope to die! She pivoted slowly and walked to the door wall. This whole thing could be over in a heartbeat. All she had to do was confess to the capital crime of Prudism.

No! A challenge had been made, and by golly, she wasn't stepping down from it. Besides, Jake was right. She'd never see those people again.

She spun around. "Okay, I'll do it," she said matter-of-factly.

"Okay?" His eyes widened in disbelief. "You'll do it? Tomorrow?"

"Which word didn't you understand?" She was feeling a little cocky now that the decision had been made. May as well. Tomorrow she'd be quaking in her boots. If she were allowed to wear them.

She held up a finger, thinking of one more condition. "I get to pick the time."

"Daylight hours?" he asked, as if suspecting a catch.

"Of course," she said, her first bright idea flying right out the window.

He clasped her hand and pumped it. "It's a deal."

Six

Friday morning, Catherine snuggled beneath the sheet, enjoying a cool breeze from the open window. Not ready to open her eyes, she listened to the palms swishing and pictured their graceful movements. It was the best night's sleep she'd had all week. She inhaled deeply, smelling the salty sea air.

Suddenly, she bolted upright in the bed and stared at the clock on the dresser. It was eight-fifteen.

"Ohhh, nooo," she moaned and darted for the bathroom. She had planned to be on the beach at the crack of dawn. She brushed her teeth and threw on her cover-up. A shower could wait until later. Breathless, she knocked on the door.

"Rise and shine. I'm going to the beach now," she called out loudly.

She heard a sleepy growl from the other side, then a gravelly, "I'm not ready."

"Okay. Deals off. You said I could pick the time." She

started for the shower, a big weight lifted from her shoulders.

Before she had time to enjoy the reprieve, Jake was at the connecting door. He opened it wide enough to stick his tousled head inside, but nothing else. For a second, she wondered if he had on briefs, shorts or nothing at all. Her gaze was riveted on the middle of the door as if magically she might see through it and know the answer. Then he yawned and she watched him rub one eye with the side of his fist, making him look like a little boy, an adorable, huggable...

"Okay. I'm awake," he said. "How much time do you want me to give you?"

Oh, two, maybe three years. She forced a smile. "Make it fifteen minutes."

Catherine walked as quickly as she could, anxious for this whole farce to be over. When she got to the beach, she was glad to find only two women sitting at the far end. They were sipping coffee from foam cups and watching a cruise ship a few miles out.

This was as good as it was going to get. Like pulling off a bandage, she decided it was best to do it quickly. She unbuttoned her cover, fingers fumbling at each hole until she was ready to rip the thing off. Finally she took one last look around, then dropped it on the lounge chair and headed for the water.

She expected it to be chilly, but it wasn't. It felt like bathwater. The bottom was clean sand, the water clear enough to see her feet. At least this part was better than she'd imagined. A lifetime of chlorinated pools had left her a little skittish about dark waters shared with living, moving objects. But as far as she could see there were no rocks, no seaweed, nor any other mysterious mush.

Relieved, she waded out through seemingly endless shallow water, taking giant steps and gazing upward. The sun, centered in the bluest sky she'd ever seen, was warm, not yet hot. A gentle wave broke on her upper thigh and she slowed her pace, luxuriating with each new step. There was something free yet secure in feeling the tepid water against her warm, bare skin. She wondered if babies felt this way in the womb. If they did, no wonder they screamed their lungs out when they were forced to leave. It felt sinfully wonderful.

Another ten yards and she dipped her shoulders below the surface and purred aloud. "Mmmm..." She might never get out. She swam to the large wooden raft anchored near the farthest buoy, taking long, lazy pulls. The salt held her high in the water and she felt the air on her backside. This was by far the best part of her vacation, she thought. Who would believe this could feel so great? She would have to thank Jake...

Jake! She reached the raft with one more long glide and then clung to the side, wiggling her toes but feeling nothing beneath them. With her free hand, she shielded her eyes and squinted back to her black cover on the white plastic chaise. It was still there, but he wasn't. Slowly she scanned the shore and felt a sudden tightness in her chest. Not because Jake was nowhere in sight, but because more than a dozen nude bathers were. And more were streaming in, staking out prime spots. *Great!* Why hadn't she set her alarm? She was supposed to be in and out of here hours ago. Without spectators. So much for the best laid plans.

She turned back to the raft, folded her arms against it and rested her head, determined not to let her anxiety spoil the moment. She'd deal with the inevitable later. Her legs floated out behind her and she closed her eyes, her body rolling with each indulgent wave. The best part was wearing no top, she thought. No strings to dig into her shoulders or elastics beneath her breasts, chafing, itching.

Yes, indeed, she sighed loudly. *A little slice of heaven.*

She pushed off the raft with a backstroke, pink nipples winking at the sun, a gentle breeze standing them firm and proud. Head tilted back, ears below water, she drifted along, listening to the muted sound of her own steady breathing. Every ounce of tension released itself as her bottom dipped deeper and she lolled in the gently undulating waves.

Then she heard the splash.

Startled, she sunk in the water. Her back to the beach and whomever was coming, she paddled back to the raft, hoping it was a woman. Maybe if she didn't acknowledge the intruder, he or she would swim away. The other end of the raft dipped lower in the water. She faced the opposite direction.

"So what do you think?"

Her wet hair whipped around behind her. "Jake! What are you doing here?"

"What does it look like I'm doing?"

He smiled at her, playing the innocent role. She sunk until her chin touched the water and then glanced down at herself.

"Relax," he said. "I can't see a thing . . . except a radiant face and beautiful shoulders." He turned away, then hoisted both elbows onto the raft behind him and stared at the beach.

Still worried about exposing too much, Catherine held on with one arm stretched to the side and turned slowly in the same direction. She tried not to notice how crowded the beach had become, but before long she was counting heads. At least she was far enough out that she couldn't see their faces, which she hoped meant they couldn't see hers. *Oh, Lordy, Lordy. What had she gotten herself into?*

"This wasn't part of the deal, you know," she finally said, trying to sound a little peeved that he was here, but not really feeling it.

"We didn't talk about anything past the part where I waited to come down."

He kept his face forward. So did she. But out of the corner of her eye, she could see his lips twitching.

"Don't worry," he added. "When you're ready to get out, just say so. I'll either leave the beach or turn my back and promise not to look. Your choice." Now he turned his head and looked at her. "You still haven't answered my question. How do you like it?"

The smile was slow in coming, but she couldn't pretend any longer. "I love it. It feels wonderful."

"I'm glad." His smile faded as he stared at her.

She felt hers slip away, too, the tightness in her chest returning. But this time she knew it had nothing to do with the distant sunbathers.

Catherine was first to look away. She pushed off and did a slow breaststroke, careful to keep her body below the surface. Still a good thirty yards from shore, she tested the depth again and felt the sand between her toes. This was better. Feet planted firmly apart, chin in the water, she spotted a pair of fish about three or four inches in length wiggle cautiously in her direction. She held perfectly still, marveling at their vivid colors of red, yellow and blue. She continued to watch, mesmerized. Then suddenly they skittered away.

Only a second passed before she saw the reason why.

Panicking, she stumbled backward, lost her footing and fell below the surface. She opened her eyes, the salt instantly stinging them. The large, dark shape slithered closer. It was more than a foot wide. Fat lips. Mottled skin. It was so long she couldn't see the end of it.

Thrusting herself upward, she screamed. She flailed her arms at Jake who was swimming wildly in her direction. Two more lengths and he was there. She threw her arms around his neck and locked her legs around his waist, fighting the urge to climb right up on his shoulders and out of the water completely.

"Is it still there?" Eyes closed, she shivered and tightened her grip. Jake was stroking her back, making shushing sounds. "Do you see it?" she asked, not masking her fear.

"It's just a baby grouper." He ran his hand down her hair. "It's leaving. Shhh . . . we're okay."

His voice was soothing and she began to feel a little safer. "It was so big . . . and *sooo* ugly," she whispered over his shoulder, her grip relaxing slightly.

"They are nasty looking buggers, aren't they?" Slowly he slid his cheek back to meet hers, his mouth softly brushing her temple.

Startled, Catherine pulled back, meeting his steady gaze. Her nose nearly touched his and she felt his warm breath on her lips. She started feeling other things now, too...her naked breasts crushed against his chest...legs, spread wide...the insides of her knees riding his hips...the insides of her thighs and the space in between pressed firmly against his belly. Her lips were parted and she was breathing faster. She knew he was going to kiss her if she didn't move.

She watched his lips. And waited.

When they finally met hers, they were tentative and she tasted their salt. Patiently Jake traced her lips with his tongue, licking the pungent taste away. Shyly she did the same, smelling his male scent mixed with the sea. When she finished, she looked cautiously into his eyes. They were dark and magnetic. She couldn't look away if she wanted to. She didn't want to.

Slowly she unlocked her legs and eased herself down the length of him, feeling the extent of his arousal. With a moan, he dug his fingers into her hips and pressed her firmly against him. Their mouths met again, urgently this time, as she felt herself melt against him, no longer sure where his body stopped and hers began. Gone was the uncertainty she felt on the dance floor Monday night, and with it that little voice that said it was impossible to feel so much so soon.

His tongue explored the recesses of her mouth and she welcomed it, trying to find a deeper, more intimate spot of her own. She lifted her hips a little higher until she felt the ridge of him against her mound. They rocked together below the water until she thought she would scream if he didn't enter her. Unexpectedly he abandoned her lips with another moan and held her tight and still, his hot breath loud in her ear as she knew hers must be in his. She could feel his heart thudding against her breasts. Or was it hers?

When one hand left her bottom, she thought he was stopping and she looked into his eyes, imploringly, not hiding her desire. He was studying her face, devouring her with hungry eyes as his finger slid gently inside her. She inhaled sharply, closing her eyes. At first, his stroke was slow and gentle. She rocked with him, encouraging each move. Then he shortened his stroke and rubbed harder. She felt selfish and wanton but couldn't stop. Her legs began trembling and she didn't think she could stand another second. Quickly he thrust his finger deeper inside her at the same time as his moist tongue filled her ear. She groaned and tightened her thighs around his hand like a vise, instantly feeling the pulse in her groin. He stretched farther yet with his finger, inserting a second one now, rotating them, rubbing and thrusting in a way she didn't know possible. Suddenly she saw shooting slivers of light behind her closed lids. Her entire body shook and she panted against his shoulder.

"Oh, Jake," she murmured. "Oh, Jake." His arm tightened on her back and she slumped against him, twitches of current shooting through her.

It took a few seconds before she noticed the pair of swimmers passing them a few yards away. She blinked, trying to focus on her surroundings, the tingling sensation below her waist not eager to abate itself.

Jake spoke softly in her ear, his warm breath sending another shiver down her spine. "It's okay, Cat. They can't see a thing."

Right now, she didn't care what they could see. She never felt so sated in her entire life. But she knew it was more than that. Much more. And the realization left her dizzy. She snuggled closer, resting her head in the crook of his neck, certain nothing wrong could feel so right. Wanting to give back in some small measure what she'd received, she shifted her weight to one side, her back to the distant beach. With one hand around his waist, the other trailed down his hip to his thigh. Unabashed, her fingers inched their way across his flat belly, grasping firmly the object of their search. He groaned. She felt his sex pulsing in her hand, the skin so taut she thought it might burst. Jake made low sounds in her ear. His legs began to tremble. It was just a matter of seconds, she thought, feeling an intimacy she had never felt before.

Out of nowhere a raft careened into her. Catherine heard Jake curse as she lost her grip and fell backward into the water. When she came up and whipped her hair from her face, she saw the culprit—that same flirt who always managed to find Jake wherever he was. The brazen woman was clinging to her raft, mouthing words of apology to Jake, ignoring Catherine's presence.

Jake glared at the intruder, not speaking, his nostrils sucking in, flaring out. There was a murderous look in his eyes as he shot her one last dismissing glare. Then he reached out to Catherine and pulled her closer.

"Are you all right?"

Catherine nodded, holding his hand but not ready to look him in the eye—afraid what she might see, yet eager to know.

They stood there a moment, neither of them speaking, staring at the same blue spot of rolling water between them, their breathing slowly returning to normal.

Ignored, the blonde paddled away mumbling something beneath her breath.

"You're shivering," Jake said when they were alone.

She glanced up, then back to the water, feeling awkward, uncertain what to say.

"Would you like to get out now?"

He sounded so caring, so giving. She felt tears start to brim. Unable to speak, she folded her arms across her breasts and nodded her head. Then it occurred to her. How was she going to get out of the water. She cast a frantic look at the crowded shore and then shivered again.

"I have an idea," Jake said as he headed in. "Wait here."

She watched his broad shoulders emerge from the water, then his narrow waist. Part of her wanted to look away when his rounded backside came into view. But she openly stared, transfixed by his perfect bronzed body as it cleared the water and walked to her black cover-up. She watched as he picked it up and moved it to the far right end of the beach.

Nonchalantly Jake found a yellow inflated raft and made his way back toward her, holding it strategically in front of him until he was waist deep in the water. Catherine thought he was doing that more for her benefit than his own. Either way, she appreciated the gesture. This whole incident could have been painfully embarrassing, but somehow he was making everything okay.

Jake pushed the raft in front of him and glided closer. There was a hint of something in his eyes. Not smug satisfaction, as she would have expected before today, but a warm, encompassing look, as if he were embracing her still.

She touched the raft as it drifted closer, feeling shy and keeping her breasts carefully concealed.

They held each other's gaze, secret words flirting behind each, but not forming sound.

Eventually Jake took charge again. "If you hold the raft vertically under your left arm, no one will see a thing," he said softly.

She glanced to her right. The brightly colored sails of four beached Sunfish provided a privacy wall between the two beaches. She looked back to Jake.

"Thank you" was all she could manage to say.

His eyes smiled before his lips. Then he turned and left. He swam to the wooden raft behind them, keeping his back to her.

With a sigh, she waded in, doing just as Jake had suggested, already missing the closeness of him and certain it could never happen again.

Jake stayed in the water until he felt like a prune. When he was certain Catherine had had plenty of time to shower and dress, he waded ashore, knotted a towel around his waist and started back for the room.

He let himself in a few minutes later, wondering if she would still be there and how she would act after what happened. The room was dark. The curtains had been pulled, but he saw her shape beneath the sheet as he stepped inside and closed the door.

Her back was to him but he was sure she wasn't asleep. He flicked on the light in the bathroom and stood in the hall, waiting for her to acknowledge his presence. She didn't move. He heaved a frustrated sigh, knowing she could hear him. Still nothing. He gave up and went into the bathroom, shutting the door with a thud.

So we're back to that game, huh? His jaw tightened as he turned the shower head up. Not waiting for the water to warm, he stepped under the cold spray, hoping it would cool off his disposition as well as his taut skin.

Damn! When would he ever learn? Women were all the same—take what they want and then leave. He lathered quickly, running the soap over his tense muscles, feeling his chest heave with each angry thought.

A few minutes later, towel secured around his middle, he crossed to the next room, found some clean clothes, dressed in a flurry and left.

He was halfway to the main hall before he slowed his pace, not sure where he was going, but wishing he was back at Alley Cat. At least there he knew his role.

He passed through the dining room and headed toward the lobby. The aroma of fresh brewed Jamaican coffee and warm pastries invited him but he wasn't hungry. Right now what he wanted more than anything was a taste of reality. He turned left off the lobby into a small room with phones, sat down in a soft upholstered chair and called Alley Cat.

After a short delay he heard the familiar voice. "Tom, how's things goin'?"

"Jake! Where are you, man?"

"Would you believe Jamaica?" Jake sunk back in the chair.

"I didn't know you were going on vacation till I got called in for extra hours."

"Yeah, well . . . it's a long story. I'll tell you all about it sometime." Jake changed the subject. "By any chance, has our friend in the pin-striped suit and wing tips been around lately?"

There was a slight pause before Tom answered. "I didn't want to say anything . . . thought it could wait till you got home. Yeah, he's been here. Acting buddy, buddy. Asking the same ol' questions."

He knew it! He should be back in Detroit taking care of business.

"Jake? You still there?"

He sighed into the receiver. "Yeah, but not for long. You working Sunday night?"

"I'm working every night."

"I'll see you then, Tom. Thanks for covering. Oh, and say hi to Sarge for me. Tell him I'll be there around seven."

Jake hung up feeling more frustrated than before. He was ready to smash his fist through the wall if he didn't work off some steam. He remembered seeing a weight room off the courtyard, somewhere near the gift shops.

When he found the room it was empty. Free-weights and numerous pieces of sophisticated equipment waited to do his bidding. He attacked each piece as if proving a point, muttering his complaints about life in general, women in particular. Sweat dripped from his hair, down his back and chest, wetting his tank top, making his running shorts cling to his skin. He pegged the weights higher, daring his arms to give way under the pressure. He grunted and pushed and grunted some more, until finally he dropped the bar and lay on his back, soaked through and breathless, and at long last tired. Head cleared, he lay on the narrow bench and thought about his predicament.

Two days left before the plane departed. There was nothing he could do about the problem at home until he got there. As far as his problem here, he would keep away from Catherine and get control of himself. He'd given in to his feelings again and look what it got him. He stood abruptly, pulling his shirt over his head and toweling himself dry with it. Then he headed for the beach.

"Mrs. Miller—or whatever your name is," he said, through clenched teeth. "You're on your own."

Catherine dried the last of her tears, sat up in the bed and blew her nose with a resounding noise.

How could she have done such a thing? With a man she hardly knew? And right out there in front of God and everybody! One thing was certain: she'd never step foot on that beach again.

But how could she manage to keep from looking Jake in the eye until they got home? The whole thing seemed hopeless.

Another tear slid down her cheek, this one more from frustration than embarrassment. She felt trapped. She lunged out of bed and went to the bathroom mirror, hoping to make something fresh out of her puffy pink face.

But her reflection told her more than she wanted to know. She was lying to herself again. Her eyes didn't say she was frustrated. Nor angry. Not even embarrassed. Her eyes said she . . . her eyes said . . .

"No!" she shouted to the glass. "It can't be." She bowed her chin to her chest and a fresh flow streaked her cheeks. She was such a fool. It could never work with a man like Jake. Besides, as soon as he found out about her inheritance . . .

She straightened her shoulders and took a deep breath. Sunday she'd be back in Detroit and this whole thing would be history. It was understandable, she rationalized, starting to repair her face. Something traumatic had happened to her last week. She had simply been looking for a way to block out the nightmare. She avoided the mirror by throwing her hair forward and brushing it vigorously, eventually tying it high on her head with a satin ribbon.

She repeated this story to herself throughout the long afternoon and early evening, each time trying to bolster her sagging spirits, and each time succeeding less and less. By the time she went back to the room to change for dinner, she'd almost talked herself into calling the airlines about an earlier flight home.

At six-thirty, Catherine zipped the back of the strapless sundress she'd found at one of the boutiques and twirled in front of the mirror just as Jake came through the door. Her eyes met his briefly then she busied herself smoothing imaginary wrinkles out of the skirt. He walked to the connecting door and she watched his legs. All of a sudden they stopped. He turned slowly and faced her.

"Look, Catherine, about this morning—"

She held up her palms cutting him off. Some things were better left undissected. This was one of them. Cautiously she let her gaze drift upward until she met his even stare. It was like looking in the mirror earlier. The truth of what she felt reflected in his dark eyes. She wanted to look away, but couldn't.

"Jake...I—"

This time he was the one to hold up a hand. "Truce?" He extended his arm, inviting a shake.

His face was still tense, she thought, no sign of the dimples she had come to... She thrust out her hand and clasped his. "Truce," she agreed. He didn't shake it as she expected but simply held it. The heat of him traveled straight to her rib cage. His thumb glided back and forth on the back of her hand, starting a familiar tingling in her lower body.

Then a frown creased his forehead. He let go of her hand and stepped back.

"If you're done in the bathroom, I'd like to shower and dress for dinner." She thought he sounded distant but then he surprised her with his next words. "Would you care to wait and join me?"

Catherine wasn't sure if he wanted her to decline the offer or accept. His eyes sent mixed signals. She looked down at her skirt and smoothed another nonexistent wrinkle. "Sure," she said, which came off sounding like *Why not? I have nothing better to do.* She heard the door shut and the shower start before she felt the muscles relax in the pit of her stomach.

Jake closed his eyes and turned his face to the warm spray. *You weak son of a bitch.* He shook his head in self-disgust and turned his back to the water. Just thirty-six more hours but he couldn't leave well enough alone.

He was still grousing to himself twenty minutes later when he emerged from his room feeling like a tourist in his white cotton drawstring pants and blue-gray batik shirt. The salesgirl had talked him into the outfit this afternoon when other things had occupied his mind. Now he felt ridiculous. Yet that was not the look Catherine was giving him. Her eyes were wide, lips parted slightly. Great lips.

She made a low whistling sound and lifted her eyebrows. "You look terrific!"

He looked down at himself, surprised. "You think so?"

"I've been in the business awhile, remember?" She was smiling, but he thought she looked embarrassed and was trying to cover. For some reason that made him relax a little. This probably wasn't any easier for her than it was for him.

"You look pretty terrific yourself," he finally said. "Turn around." She pirouetted in front of him, the skirt flaring higher above her knees. He thought about joking and asking her how she kept the thing up without straps, but then he remembered her full breasts against his chest this morning and decided against it.

"Ready to go?" He stepped closer and proffered a raised elbow. She took it and smiled up at him with those damnable blue eyes of hers.

"I'm ready if you are."

Seven

The Italian restaurant just beyond the main hall proved a popular Friday night spot. Guests seeking a change of pace dressed less casually, ordered off the menu and relaxed to the sounds of classical music.

The earliest reservation was for eight-thirty. They took it, then stood there eyeing each other awkwardly, wondering what to do for the next hour and a half.

Jake snapped his fingers. "I know just the place to go. Follow me."

Catherine lingered a moment, admiring the fit of his white pants as he walked away, then she scurried to catch up.

"Where we going?" she asked, short of breath.

"Did you ever notice that little stucco building with the brick walk leading to the door?" He moved with a long, fast stride and she nearly ran to keep up.

"The one with the green wrought iron benches in front?" They rounded the corner and it came into view.

"Yep. That's the place," he said, pointing to the right.

Catherine followed him inside wondering when he had been here. The door closed behind her and the air-conditioning gave her a sudden chill. She rubbed her hands on her bare shoulders and surveyed the rooms, pleasantly surprised at what she saw. In front of her was a highly polished mahogany bar, a smiling Jamaican drying glasses and talking quietly with a guest leaning on the counter. Beyond was a sunken area with a beautiful black baby grand in the middle of the floor. An upholstered bar and high stools with dark wooden arms bordered three sides. The piano bench was empty, but from somewhere nearby came the sound of a concert grand. As much as she enjoyed the reggae beat, the change felt instantly soothing.

To the left was a huge saltwater aquarium, at least fifteen feet long, filled with more of the beautiful creatures she'd enjoyed earlier today. Behind it was a room that looked like a library, with small game tables strategically placed. A couple on the other side played backgammon and sipped cocktails. While she took this all in, Jake wandered over to the aquarium.

Catherine walked down the carpeted steps and joined him. "They're beautiful, aren't they?"

Jake answered in a hushed voice. "So much more colorful than freshwater fish. I'd always wished I had a chance..." His voice trailed off and he didn't finish.

"A chance to what?" Catherine asked gently, suddenly wanting to know more about this complex man she roomed with. He was silent for the longest time and she wasn't sure he had heard her question. But then he answered in an odd way.

"I used to have a sailboat." His expression changed, as though fond memories swirled around in his head. "Always wished I could sail her south, somewhere near the Virgin Islands, in salt water. Dock her in places like this...snorkel, find fish as colorful and interesting as these..."

"Why didn't you?" She saw his jaw muscles flex and knew her mistake.

He turned his face to hers and spoke through clenched teeth. "Because I lost her to a woman. Any more questions?"

Yes. There were several. How could he afford such a boat? But even more pressing, what woman? And how did he lose something so valuable to her? There was so much she didn't know about this man. And suddenly she wanted to know it all. Yet she sensed she'd better tread lightly.

"Could we get some wine and sit down for a while?" she asked gently. She saw his jaw relax and he looked as though he was about to apologize for snapping at her. "Come on," she smiled, hooking her elbow around his. "Buy me a drink."

Jake ordered a Red Stripe for himself and a Chablis for Catherine and then carried both to the piano bar. They sat on stools in the center.

Catherine sipped her wine and closed her eyes, enjoying the wraparound sound system. It felt as though music was coming from everywhere yet nowhere, seeping into her every pore. If there had been a bed here, she'd have been in it— lying on her side, cuddled with Jake, her head on his shoulder, his lips in her hair...

"Are you still here?" he said, breaking her trance.

She could feel the flush on her cheeks and was grateful for the sunburn. She opened her eyes slowly and looked at him. He was studying her face and smiling.

"Tell me about her, Jake...please," she said softly.

"The woman or the boat?" He smirked and took a hearty swallow from the long neck.

"Both." He stared at the label, rolling the bottle between his palms. She couldn't tell if he was trying to figure out where to start or whether to tell her at all. She held her breath and waited.

"I dropped out of college my junior year," he started. "My dad needed help. Or at least that's the excuse I used at the time. I had a pretty bad attitude about everything back then." He looked at Catherine out of the corner of his eye, cocking a corner of his mouth in that roguish look of his. "Unlike my charming personality now." He laughed into his bottle before taking another swig. "Anyway...I'd been working long hours since I was a kid. Always found it easy to save, since I'm not much of a consumer, don't really need...things. Except I always wanted a sailboat. One of my dad's friends had a boat and took me out on it every chance we got...taught me everything there was to know about sailing."

There was a more peaceful look on Jake's face than Catherine remembered seeing before. She sipped her wine and leaned back in the chair, enjoying this side of Jake more than she thought was wise, but feeling too comfortable to fight it.

"After the man died, his family called...wanted to know if I was interested in buying the boat. I told them how much I had in my savings—which I was sure wasn't enough—and the next thing I knew, I owned it."

Catherine pictured him on the water, his face turned into the wind, the sun leaving little white lines at the corners of his eyes from squinting, his long, sandy hair blowing free...

"Then along came Sally," he said, finishing his beer and setting it down with a thud. "She was a cocktail waitress with big dreams and big..." He looked at Catherine and grinned. "Well, anyway, she dangled her bait and I bit." He shook his head from side to side. "She reeled me in with about as much resistance as a minnow." He harrumphed, then the grin disappeared. He folded his arms across his chest and leaned back, rocking the stool on two legs.

"And then?" Catherine asked, impatient for the next part.

Jake looked her straight in the eye before he answered. "And then, like a fool, I married her."

He was gauging her reaction and she knew it, but she couldn't conceal her surprise. Married? Was she in Jamaica with a married man?

"It didn't last a year," he added, and she heard the breath she'd been holding escape. She took a quick sip of wine, trying to mask her relief as Jake continued.

"That mistake cost me dearly."

"The boat," she said, putting it all together.

"Not just any boat." He corrected her. *"Cat's Meow!"*

Wine was still in her mouth when the laugh caught at the back of her throat.

"Cat's Meow?" She began to cough and laugh all at the same time, pressing a napkin to her mouth and fighting for control. Jake patted her on the back, trying not to laugh himself. When she finally stopped, or thought she had, she looked at his dimpled cheeks and giggled again behind the napkin.

"I'm sorry," she said, trying to keep a straight face. "I can imagine how much..." she couldn't say it, "how much your *boat* meant to you."

Jake smiled at her, looking amused at her reaction.

"You don't like the name *Cat's Meow?*"

She thought he was teasing her now, but she couldn't be sure so she took the safe road. "No, it's not that at all. It's a very... cute name."

He cocked an eyebrow. "Cute?"

She braved another sip of wine. "Yeah... cute." She studied his face over the rim of her wineglass. He didn't seem angry or offended. If she didn't know better, she'd think he was actually starting to have fun. But how could that be? Such a serious subject and all. She set her wine down, deciding it and her empty stomach must be the reason for this sudden giddiness.

"It's Sally you should be laughing at," he said out of the blue.

"Sally? What's so funny about Sally?"

"Think about it." He leaned an elbow on the bar and turned to face her. "What woman in her right mind would walk around calling herself Sally Alley?" A low chuckle started at the back of his throat, then burst from his lips with a hearty laugh.

Catherine watched his face light up as he laughed. She laughed along with him, wondering if this was the first time he saw any humor in his past.

"So tell me something," he said when he regained his composure. "I'm curious. What exactly do the initials 'TJ' stand for?"

Catherine laughed again, already knowing what his reaction would be. "Terrance Jerome." As she suspected, he slapped his leg and laughed louder.

"Well there, you see? We both should have known better."

Catherine continued laughing as he took her hand and led her back to the restaurant. Along the way, a silly game began drifting through her mind.

Sally Alley...Catherine Alley...Cat Alley...Alley Cat...

Before they reached their destination, the giddiness diminished, replaced by the same nagging feeling she'd felt earlier—staring at her reflection in the mirror.

During dinner at Jake's prodding, Catherine told him about her family, how Dad owned a brokerage firm while Mom busied herself with gardening and charities. And like Jake, how she was an only child who always wished she'd had brothers and sisters. She surprised him when she said she was considering working with the homeless once she left her job. Noble, he thought, but how did she think she'd pay the bills? Remembering her reaction on the boat, he kept his thoughts to himself.

When she mentioned TJ, though, Jake was even more surprised. He would have guessed Studly was the last subject she'd want to discuss.

"Our parents were lifelong friends so we knew each other from childhood," Catherine began, then confused him further with her next question.

"Did you ever have a dog?"

Now where did that come from? Women's minds would always be a mystery to him. "Sure," he said, trying to figure out where this was headed.

"When I was twelve years old I had a miniature dachshund that was supposed to sleep on the floor next to my bed, but she always managed to slip beneath my covers as soon as Mom kissed me good-night and left the room."

Jake watched her toy with her wineglass looking as though she might cry.

"When Heidi broke her back and had to be put to sleep, I thought I'd die, too. I barely ate for weeks and it was almost a year before my mother talked me out of sleeping with Heidi's collar under my pillow. Maybe she was only a dog, but even now, it still hurts to think about her."

Jake remembered his collie dying of old age and understood Catherine's glassy eyes. Still, why was she telling him this now?

"A thought struck me as odd this week. Seventeen years after losing Heidi, I miss her more than TJ."

She looked up and Jake knew she was watching his reaction. He did his best to show none. Now that he knew what she was saying, he wanted her to finish.

"As much as I'd like to deny it, there's only one explanation." She stared at the twisting wineglass in her hands. "I never loved TJ."

Jake didn't like the celebration that was starting in his gut and moving south. *Great! She cleansed her soul.* Still, he had to remember—it had nothing to do with him.

"Oh, I loved TJ's family." Catherine prattled on, more to herself than Jake. "I loved his good looks and charming ways. I even loved the idea he was a successful attorney."

At this, Jake almost interjected a snide remark, but with great restraint he remained silent.

"But I didn't love TJ." She looked up at Jake with a "There! I said it aloud" kind of look, pleased with herself for her candor. Then appearing embarrassed, she lowered her gaze and added more softly, "At least not the way a wife should love a husband."

Jake didn't know what she expected him to say so he waited to see if she was done. After an awkward silence she spoke again.

"I guess it was a selfish thing to do—taking off the way I did." She glanced up and down quickly, signaling it was time for him to comment.

"Hey, who would have been okay with a scene like that?" he said. "I don't think anyone would fault you." They'd be too busy lambasting Studly. Jake watched Catherine relax, looking pleased with his few words of support. Then she laughed.

"Mother may have taught me to cover my mouth when I sneezed and what silverware to use, but she never said, 'If you catch your husband messing with another woman on your wedding night, here's the proper way to act.'"

Jake laughed along with Catherine, feeling a comfort level that was both foreign and frightening.

"I'm just glad Granddad wasn't there to witness the debacle. He was the type that might have castrated TJ on the spot." Catherine flashed a rueful smile as if the idea wasn't half bad.

Finally Jake held up both hands as if someone had poked a pistol in his back. "Wait a minute. I'm confused. Who exactly is this grandfather you talk about?"

Now Catherine looked puzzled. "You mean you don't know?"

"Am I supposed to?"

"Well, you were at the wedding, I just assumed..."

Jake studied her face. She seemed to be debating whether to tell him. "The way you look, you'd think he was a bank robber or something. Just spit it out. It can't be that bad." Jake winked at her and started to take another bite of banana cream pie. His fork was halfway to his mouth when she answered.

"My paternal grandfather is...was Marshall Mason."

Jake dropped his fork and stared openmouthed at Catherine. "No sh...no kidding? *The* Marshall Mason? Department store mogul?" Catherine nodded and kept her eyes cast down. Jake picked up his coffee and drank, digesting the news.

So *that* was her name. Catherine *Mason*. He didn't want to tell her he hadn't remembered. Even if he had, he wouldn't have guessed she was part of a dynasty.

He sat his cup down and looked at her as if seeing her for the first time. Besides being beautiful, he noticed other things now. The way she held herself, her perfectly manicured fingers, the raised pinkie now that she lifted her cup to her lips. He could tell at the wedding her family had a little dough but Grandpa had to be filthy rich. The clues had been right under his nose but he'd missed them all.

What he didn't miss was the sad look on Catherine's face. She looked as though she might cry any second. Jake pushed out his chair and stood, bringing Catherine's head up with a start.

"Come on." He reached out and took her hand, tugging her from her chair. "Let's get out of here."

They strolled through the courtyard, down the winding maze of jungle foliage and passed the lighted tennis courts, all without a word. Jake wondered if by his silence she might be thinking her news made a difference. In a way, it did. That, and her very proper Presbyterian wedding. Both made it easier to understood where she got that uptight, prudish side of her, and how guilty and embarrassed she must have felt after their little escapade in the water. Nude sunbathing and that kind of water sport were probably never discussed, let alone practiced, at whatever preppie school Catherine must have attended. Considering her background and what Studly had done to her, she'd been a pretty good sport this week, he thought, as they approached the door to their suite.

The sun had gone down and he hadn't even noticed. When he glanced at his watch it was almost ten. After a day of water, sun and fresh air, he was usually ready to call it a night by this time. Tonight he was restless.

A warm, humid breeze drifted through the courtyard, stirring a potent blend of eucalyptus and the orchidlike flowers that sprouted from everywhere. He inhaled deeply, hearing again the eerie chorus of crickets.

"Have you ever heard such a racket?" he asked, breaking the silence.

"No, I haven't."

He watched the moonlight play on her face as he retrieved the key.

"The first night we were here, I thought it was some kind of mechanical malfunction. It was so loud and steady—"

Jake spun around in front of her, cutting off her words. "Let's go find the whirlpool," he said with newfound energy. When she hesitated, he threw open the door. "Go get your suit on. I'll get mine." She smiled faintly, seeming to warm to the idea.

A few minutes later, from the other side of the closed door, Jake called out. "It's supposed to hold three hundred people. It shouldn't be hard to find." He shed his clothes in a heap and pulled on his damp swim trunks. "I'm ready when you are."

Another minute passed and then Catherine opened the door. He tried not to stare at her white bikini, which contrasted sharply with her golden brown skin, but it was difficult.

"Should we take towels?" she asked.

"I'm sure there'll be some there. Let's go." He took her hand and she didn't resist. As an afterthought, he grabbed a prize-winning bottle of rum off the dresser.

They wandered to the far end of the property, the only place Jake hadn't explored, and found the irregular-shaped pool. Steam swirled above the massive surface. Two couples were nestled close to each other at one end, their whispers low, almost reverent. Jake and Catherine headed for the other side.

Patio lights, discreetly placed at the base of a few palms, highlighted a flurry of bromeliads and larger, leafy plants that looked like rubber trees. Off to one side was a self-serve counter, complete with towels, plastic tumblers, ice and a variety of soft drinks in a dispenser.

Catherine sat on the edge of the pool and dangled her feet while Jake helped himself to two Cokes and towels. He came back and sat next to her, handing over a drink. He uncapped the rum, poured himself a shot, and used his index finger as a stir. Then he hoisted the bottle in front of her.

"Sure. Why not?" she said, seeming more relaxed. He mixed her drink and set the bottle down behind them, feeling like a pimply-faced kid on his first date.

"So... where did you go to school?" Now there was an original opener.

"University of Michigan. And you?"

"Michigan State."

"Ahhh," she said, acknowledging the age-old rivalry with a single word and a mischievous twitch at the corner of her mouth. "What did you study?" she asked, slowly slipping into the churning water.

"You're not going to believe this." He joined her, sitting on the ledge several inches below the surface. "Computer programming."

"Really?" She seemed surprised. He thought about saying he couldn't find a class in bartending, but decided not to be a smart-ass. Things were starting to smooth out. He didn't want to press his luck. He thought her next question would be "How did you end up tending bar?" but it was her turn to surprise him.

"Jake . . . how did you come to be at my wedding?" She was looking at him suspiciously, as if it occurred to her he might have been a party crasher.

He chuckled and hooked his elbows over the edge of the pool behind him, trying to figure out where to start his story and how much to tell. He took a sip of rum and Coke before answering.

"I have Aunt Helen to thank for that." He paused again, questioning the wisdom of opening this subject at all. She'd only want to know more. Still, for some reason it seemed like the right thing to do, especially after all she'd told him at dinner. Uncertain, he proceeded.

"Aunt Helen was supposed to go with a friend from work but she got a migraine at the last minute and I was called to the rescue. Aunt Helen doesn't drive."

"And who exactly is Aunt Helen? I mean . . . should I know her?"

"She's the bookkeeper at your dad's office."

Catherine thumped her palm against her temple. "Of course. Helen Alley! I can't remember the last time I heard Dad use her last name. But Helen . . ." she shook her head, dumbstruck by the connection. "Dad's spoken kindly of Helen for years—says she's the best employee he's ever had—always on time, never sick, friendly . . . and extremely efficient."

"That's Aunt Helen." Jake smiled, enjoying the praise. Aunt Helen had been more like a mother than an aunt. Without thinking, he told Catherine that.

"Are you saying she raised you?"

Jake pulled himself up on the edge and drained his glass. "I've had enough of this heat. Wanna go down to the beach?"

"Sure." She held out her hand and he gave it a tug. "But let's get more Coke." She jiggled her empty glass. "This stuff is pretty good."

Catherine refilled glasses while Jake grabbed extra towels and together they padded barefoot down the narrow path to the beach.

A full moon mirrored the surface of the gently rolling sea, a lone schooner silhouetted against the night. Small waves broke and tumbled in, sometimes reaching their feet.

They lay side by side on towels near the water's edge, hands locked behind their heads, gazing at the cloudless sky. They had found and named every constellation they could think of before falling into a companionable silence.

Catherine glanced sideways to see if Jake was still awake. His eyes were open and his face seemed relaxed, content.

"Have you ever seen such a magnificent sky?" he asked in a low, husky voice.

Catherine turned on her side, propping her head with a bent arm, and studied his handsome profile. When she didn't answer, he turned his face and met her steady gaze.

"What?" he asked.

"I was just wondering if you were ever going to answer my question," she said, unable to contain her curiosity any longer.

"What question was that?" He looked back at the stars.

He knew very well which question, she thought, but she repeated it anyway. "Did your aunt raise you?" And if so, where were your parents? she wanted to add but waited. She counted four waves break at her feet before he heaved a sigh.

"You sure you want to hear all this?"

"Yes. I do." She was surprised how true her words were, how much she yearned to know everything about this secretive man she had come to care for more than she thought was wise.

"I'll skip the early years," he started. "They were pretty ordinary...school, skinned knees, Scouts. My parents seemed happy enough with each other, I guess. I never paid that close attention, thinking they'd be there forever. They worked a lot of hours at the bar together. Sometimes I'd go with them, fill napkin holders, play with swizzle sticks, that kind of exciting stuff." He glanced at her as if expecting her to be bored. Satisfied that she wasn't he continued, the smile fading from his eyes.

"Then Dad was called up from the Reserves and sent to Nam. The time he was gone seemed forever. I remember asking Mom 'How much longer?' so many times that she finally gave me my own calendar. She had me mark the end and then count backward. Every day that passed I put a big X through it and lowered the number." He sat up and locked his arms around his bent knees. Catherine lay perfectly still. His tension was almost palpable. She wanted to hear the rest but feared the mood that had come over him.

"There were twenty-eight days left when Mom told me to add another six months...and maybe it would be longer than that. She never had the guts to tell me why. By then, she spent all her time at work...or so she said," he added cynically. "It was Aunt Helen who finally told me."

Catherine sat up slowly. Hesitantly she placed a hand on his back, half expecting him to shrug it off. When he didn't she began stroking his warm skin, resting her cheek against his rigid arm. He continued in a husky voice, almost as if she weren't there.

"It was nearly a year before he came home." Jake's voice cracked and he turned his face away. "Eight months later my mother was gone. She never left a note or said goodbye. She just left." He sat very still, staring at the sea.

A lump rose in Catherine's throat and she couldn't speak. She wished she could think of the right thing to say that would ease his pain. The scars seemed so deep, she wondered if they would ever heal.

Finally he turned to her, studying her face for the longest time before he spoke. "That's how I came to live with my aunt." Catherine stared at his lips, waiting for the rest to come out. When it didn't, she asked tentatively.

"And your father?"

His dark eyes brightened at long last. "He's an incredible man. After all he's been through, he always seems at peace with himself . . . happy actually."

Forgetting her resolve not to see Jake once they got home, she heard the words pass her lips, knowing they were true. "I'd like to meet him sometime."

He caught her hand sliding down his arm and squeezed it, his tender gaze searing right through her when he smiled. "You already have."

Eight

——

"**S**arge is your father?" She pictured the man in the wheelchair at Alley Cat and now everything started to slip into place.

"That's the guy." Jake laid back down and stared at the sky.

Catherine rolled on her stomach beside him and leaned her chin on the palm of her hand. She watched his face. More was churning behind those dark eyes.

"I wish I could have seen him that year he was in the VA hospital," Jake said. "But he was in California and I was in school in Michigan."

His wistful look brought the lump back to her throat.

"After Aunt Helen told me about his...his legs, I started drawing funny cartoons for him. When he could write back, he told me the pictures were hanging on the walls all around his bed, that they helped a lot."

Catherine felt a tear roll down her cheek, but she didn't wipe it away, afraid any motion might break the spell. For some reason, she was certain he had never talked about these things before and she didn't want him to stop.

"He was kind of quiet when he got home…just sat in his chair and stared a lot. Sometimes I'd catch him watching my mother…with a sad, curious look. Now that I think back, he probably knew she was leaving long before she actually did. She was a very beautiful woman—" His jaw muscles flexed. "With a lot of need and not much to give."

With that single sentence, Catherine thought she'd learned more about Jake Alley than anything she had seen or heard all week. Maybe more than he let anyone else ever know. She slid closer, resting her cheek against his shoulder, draping an arm across his heaving chest. She could feel his heart thudding. A wave broke and she felt the warm foam stretch up to her knees and then wash back out. Her hand trailed over the downy hair on his chest and she could feel the tension in him beginning to ebb.

They lay there, not speaking, the water beginning to tickle her inner thighs. The seductive sounds of distant reggae wafted over the breaking waves and she felt his arm circle her back, nudging her closer. Without thinking, she slid a leg over his, bringing her bent knee up high on his rock-hard thighs.

A moment later, when he rolled her on top of him, she lifted her head and met his soulful gaze. There was an intensity there she'd never seen, a tumultuous mix of uncertainty and need, a desire for more than the intermingling of their bodies.

Purposefully she inched her body higher. Even through their suits, she felt the full measure of his arousal, hot and hard against her belly. She knew what was going to happen if she didn't stop, but she couldn't leave him now if she tried. He stroked her hair tenderly and whispered in a low, hoarse voice.

"Cat, Cat…what am I going to do about you?"

For a fleeting second, she remembered him calling her that before. He couldn't possibly know that those closest to her called her Cat. The mere sound of his lips forming that word reassured her she could trust him as he drew her closer.

Their mouths came together, warm and wet, soft and giving, as if they knew each other well but desired a new intimacy, borne of caring, but quickly growing to hungry need.

His hands clasped her backside and her knees dropped to the wet towel on either side of his hips. She pulled away from him slowly, not wanting to leave his lips, but eager to shed the fabric that separated her flesh from his. Holding his steady gaze, she removed her top, tossing it aside, surprised that she felt no shame. His gaze dropped to her exposed breasts, his hands catching up a moment later as he fondled each, raising the rosy centers with a deft flick of his thumbs. Quickly he shrugged out of his trunks and eased her bottoms off her.

A wave broke against her spread legs, the seminal scent of salt water awakening the last of her senses. Her lips parted on a moan and she gave into the heat of the night, lowering herself to him. She kissed his chest, nibbling lightly down his stomach toward an act that was foreign to her yet seemed so natural, so right. The water rolled higher wetting the ends of her hair that fell over her shoulder and swirled around his hips. When her tongue flicked his velvety head, she tasted salt, but didn't care.

Taking him into her mouth, she felt him pulse against her wet lips, his low moan merging with another breaking wave. The water ebbed and he pulled her to him, his lips hungrier than before. His wet fingers delved into her center, probing, tormenting as they had this morning. Their bodies began rocking in a primitive dance, fueled by the sounds of steel drums and steadily slapping waves, waves that came harder and faster, like her own hot breath.

Unable to wait another moment, Catherine raised her hips and Jake positioned her above him, the tip of his rigid sex meeting the soft cleft of hers. By measured degrees he entered her, until finally she impaled herself on him, taking him fully inside her. Her body undulated in a rhythm all its own, shivers of pleasure streaking through her as again and again the ridge of him rubbed her most sensitive spot. His tongue moved in her mouth, matching the rhythm of their bodies and her moan was lost on the night's thick air. Not even the water that rolled across her back could extinguish the flame that spread and burned inside her. The muscles in her legs and abdomen contracted and she felt her world spin out of control, no part of her able to fight the sensations that streaked through her, nor the cry that escaped her lips. In one swift movement, Jake rolled her to her back and plunged deeper, burying every wondrous inch of himself inside her as if seeking a closer union. He thrust repeatedly, each time burying himself to the hilt as her tremors came again and again, blood pumping wildly through her veins.

Suddenly Jake withdrew. His brow pursed and his jaw muscles tightened as he held his breath, then let it out with a long, low sigh. Finally he dropped to her side.

Catherine nibbled on his shoulder, missing the full feeling of him inside her. Careless as it may have been, she wished he had spilled himself into her and that she could feel his hot seed between her legs. And as gluttonous as it may seem, she knew she wanted more of this man. Tonight.

"You know what I'd like more than anything?" he asked.

She barely heard him speak, her own jagged breathing matching his. "No, what?" she asked, finding it hard to concentrate with no blood left in her head.

"A nice, soft bed."

With a devilish smile she stood, legs still trembling, and held out her hand.

At dawn Saturday morning Catherine nudged from beneath Jake's protective arm. Slipping into her cover-up she tiptoed out onto the patio. She inhaled deeply, enjoying the intoxicating scent of the flowering bushes that bordered three sides. Another gorgeous day. Their last, she thought sadly. But leaving this tropical paradise was not what weighed on her mind this morning.

In front of her was a white wrought-iron bench. She sat on it gingerly, feeling its hardness against her tender, swollen flesh—another reminder of what she would be leaving behind when she left this island. Jake had been gentle and caring, far more concerned with pleasing her than himself. It had seemed so right at the moment. She hadn't been thinking of the future. That was the problem, she chastised herself. She hadn't been thinking at all. Only feeling. Feeling and enjoying all the wondrous things he . . .

A red-billed hummingbird settled on a branch a few yards away. She watched it awhile, trying to set her mind and heart free. But all she felt was a heavy sadness. What about all her plans for the future—including her resolve not to have another relationship until she got her life together? Jake was a good man, from the little she knew, but it was too soon. There was so much she had to do first. And so much he still didn't know about her. Well, at least one very important thing that was bound to change everything. Behind her she heard Jake roll over and let out a sleepy sigh.

He knew who her grandfather was now. She'd seen that familiar awe in his face—a normal enough reaction. Still, he thought she was merely a buyer for the store, living on her own wages. She never thought of herself as a snob, but the truth was Jake was a struggling bartender whose only visible asset was a topless Jeep.

She didn't care that he had so little, but sooner or later, it would surely bother him that she had so much.

Once he knew the extent of her inheritance how could he not change?

She stared beyond the palm trees to the sea as painful lessons from her past played out in front of her like a haunting hologram. Her parents had wanted her to attend a private school where her peers would be from similar backgrounds. Catherine insisted on the local public school, certain her family's wealth would not be the measure with which she'd be judged. The first six years she'd blended in fine, but then the sleep-overs started with girlfriends, and dances meant boys coming to the house. And with age, clothes became more important to both sexes. If anyone had thought her last name was a coincidence, by the time a few saw her with Granddad at Mason's everyone knew the truth.

Then everyone and everything changed. Girls who'd never spoken to her before were hinting at discounts on clothes. Boys were queuing up at the door as if she was a free pass to Disneyland. One by one, all those she'd called friends had wanted something from her, so much so that one day she'd cried on her father's shoulder. "Why couldn't we be poor like everyone else?" Dad had stroked her hair and laughed softly, telling her Bloomfield Hills children were far from poor.

Nonetheless, the next year she enrolled at Kingswood Academy, an exclusive girls' school at Cranbrook. Her parents had been right. Girls of similar means weren't impressed with her last name. Many out-of-staters had never heard of Mason's. Through it all Catherine had learned a valuable lesson.

People *without* viewed people *with* in a whole different light. They didn't see beyond the money. Not only didn't they know the real Catherine Mason, but they didn't care.

Jake walked out onto the patio and Catherine pulled herself back to the present with a jolt. She wasn't ready to look him in the eye, let alone try to explain why this had to end. Here and now. *Damn.* She needed more time to think.

"Morning-after regrets?" he asked, sitting beside her on the bench.

Regrets that they had made love? Not once but three times. No, not in the sense he meant. But yes, she had regrets. Regrets that it could never be more than one glorious night.

When she didn't answer, Jake cupped her chin in his hand and turned her face to his. "Cat...what is it?"

She wished he wouldn't call her that. Not now. His tender gaze probed her face for an answer and for a crazy second she thought about telling him the rest of the story. But then all this would change, just as it had in school. He would never look at her the way he was looking at her right this moment. Better that she have last night—and this look—to remember and cherish, than to tarnish it with foolish confessions in a moment of weakness. Besides, the timing was all wrong. She had to be a whole person first, before she gave any part of herself away.

Unable to endure the nearness of him another second, she stood and walked inside, only to be greeted by the scent of their love-stained sheets. She fought the urge to throw herself on them and cry, loud and hard, until there were no more tears left. Instead she stumbled by the foot of the bed and headed for the bathroom. If only the plane were leaving this morning instead of tomorrow. What could she say to him until then? How could she be in the same room with this man for twenty-four hours and not succumb to the truth, let alone his touch? She felt his warm hands on her shoulders and she jumped. His fingers trailed down her arms as he gently kissed the curve of her neck.

Instinctively she jerked free, regretting her reaction the moment it happened. She felt him back away, making that small harrumphing noise she'd heard him make before when he was angry. More than anything, she wanted to turn and throw her arms around his neck, feel his body pressed to hers, feel the warmth and security of his embrace, the soft whisper of her name on his lips.

But she didn't. She couldn't.

If she even as much as turned around, she knew her resolve would wither, then disintegrate completely. The easy way out was to let him think poorly of her, let him be angry. She disgusted herself. What must he be thinking? But there was no other solution in sight. With all the strength she could muster, she walked into the bathroom and locked the door behind her.

Jake shoved his legs into his cold, damp swim trunks left on the floor the night before and strode out the door, slamming it hard behind him. He ground his teeth all the way to the beach.

Just when he thought this time was different, Catherine proved him wrong. Just when he began to think it was unfair to lump all women with his mother and Sally, along comes another long-legged beauty, squeezing feelings from him as if he was a piece of ripe fruit, feelings he wished had never surfaced.

Damn! What a stupid bastard he was.

He waded out a few yards and then dived into the cool morning sea, swimming hard and fast beyond the wooden raft and then the buoys farther out. Winded, he rolled on his back and floated, his chest heaving, his mind welcoming the distraction. When he glanced at the deserted beach and pictured Catherine on top of him in the sand, he dived again and repeated the exercise.

Finally, his lungs begging for relief, he dragged himself ashore, dropped on a chaise lounge and stared at the vast expanse of the Caribbean that spread itself in front of him. The cruise ship he'd spotted yesterday was gone. In its place was a lone catamaran headed his way. He watched it awhile before his gaze drifted to the row of Sunfish to his left.

Sprinting the distance to the small thatched-roofed building up the beach, Jake signed the official form, took the proffered life belt, and headed for the nearest boat.

A half mile from shore, he began to relax. At least out here there was no chance of running into Catherine. When he got hungry, he'd go in. But except for meals, he just might spend the day out here. He noticed again the small island to the west. A perfect spot to explore, swim off its beach if he felt like it.

His frustration seemed to diminish the farther out he sailed. With the sheet in his hand he felt in control, knowing what response to expect, each movement predictable and honest.

Yes, sir! The only female worth trusting was one with a hull below and a sail above. Never again would he let his guard down.

He tugged at the sheet, the wind billowing into the canvas, and he picked up speed, feeling the rush he always got as the bow sluiced through the water.

Awhile later when he began to tack, he glanced at the empty space on the other side of the cockpit and pictured Catherine—her hair blowing free in the wind, a smile on her lips, those full, tender, tasty lips.

He cursed into the wind and completed the tack, letting his mind ask the questions his heart didn't have the guts to face earlier.

Why had she changed so abruptly? Last night she was warm and giving. This morning, cold and indifferent. He didn't think she had too much to drink. They had put a dent in the rum, but that was after a big dinner. The only explanation he could come up with was their diverse backgrounds—a fact that she may have ignored in the moonlight but couldn't in the harsh light of day. In spite of the fact that they both attended college, he was still blue collar at heart, while Catherine was definitely white. Starched white and lacy, at that.

A sardonic smile tugged at his lips. Her parents couldn't be over the shock of the aborted wedding yet. What would they have said if she'd introduced them to a new bartender boyfriend? Of course, if she'd stuck around awhile longer he would have told her he wasn't just the bartender at Alley Cat. He was the owner. And that hadn't been his only source of income, either. Not that any of that could possibly matter to someone as highfalutin as Ms. Mason.

Besides, his assets were a far cry smaller than his liabilities these days. If Catherine knew how much money he owed Sally come November, she'd run for cover, certain family money was what attracted him in the first place. As much as it stung at the moment, maybe Catherine's change of behavior was for the best. A woman in his life right now could only make matters worse than they already were, if that was possible.

Suddenly he remembered her remark when he asked if she'd ever been to Alley Cat. *A nice place for beauticians to meet wanna-be cowboys.* At the time the dig had cut him to the quick and he'd almost blurted out that the place was his. Now he was glad he hadn't. She knew far too much about him already.

He began another tack still muttering to himself. If he hadn't been so blind he would've seen Ms. Mason for who she was that first night. A blue-blooded, selfish, spoiled...snob. He swore again and completed the tack, repeating his vow to forget her and concentrate on the bigger problem—how to pay off Sally before he lost Alley Cat and all he'd fought so hard to keep.

* * *

At ten Sunday morning the porter knocked on the door and Catherine opened it. Her carryon and a new canvas duffel sat ready and waiting inside.

"Is this all, ma'am?" He looked at the two small bags.

"There's another in the next room." She motioned over her shoulder and then stepped around him, eager to leave before Jake came out. She'd showered and dressed early and spent most of the morning reading her book over breakfast, afraid to look up. If Jake had been there, she hadn't noticed. So far they'd been able to avoid each other completely.

She strode down the walk to the main hall and turned left for the reception area, happy to see the shuttle bus already there with other luggage being loaded aboard. At least they wouldn't be alone for the two-hour ride to the airport, she thought, approaching the bus. If her luck held out, maybe there would be extra seats on the plane so she could sit as far away from Jake as possible.

She spotted an empty space in the rear of the bus next to a woman who was staring out the window, looking as though she were sad to be leaving. Under normal circumstances, Catherine would be, too. But this morning, more than anything, she wanted her feet planted firmly on Michigan soil, back to reality and the new life she had planned.

Catherine slid in beside the woman, eliminating any chance that Jake would try sitting next to her. Through the window, she caught a glimpse of him rounding the front of the vehicle. Quickly she pulled her book from her purse and began to read, the fluttering in her stomach beginning anew.

The mere sight of him was unsettling. What must he think of her after, after... Heat crawled up her neck to her cheeks. She heard shoes on the steps and buried her face behind the pages.

Once the bus began moving she stole a peek up front. He sat in the first row on the opposite side, staring at the passing scenery. She noticed his hair seemed more blond after a week in the sun. His neck was deeply bronzed, as were his arms, contrasting sharply with his white short-sleeved shirt.

Her heart was in her throat again. A burning moisture brimmed at her eyelids. She was surprised there were any tears left after yesterday. She looked back to her book, the words blurry.

The woman next to her seemed in a world of her own, a godsend Catherine appreciated. She didn't think she could speak now if her life depended on it. The lump had grown larger, a sob wanting out so badly she wasn't sure she could control it. She sucked in air and swallowed hard. The ache abated slightly but a hot tear escaped, trailing down her cheek. Quickly she brushed it away and closed her eyes.

Had she gone completely mad? How could she feel so strongly about a man she'd only known one week? It wasn't at all logical.

But then, she reminded herself, emotions never were.

Catherine waited until everyone else had cleared the gate before she walked up the steps and boarded the plane. Her preassigned seat was "6A." Anything forward of that would do, or a coach seat in back if need be. Only if it were the last seat on the plane would she sit next to Jake Alley.

Her worries proved groundless. The first row was completely vacant. She stowed her carryon overhead and then settled into the window seat. No sooner was she buckled in than the plane began taxiing down the runway.

A few minutes later as they began their ascent, Catherine took in one last view of the Caribbean, the bluest ocean she'd ever seen, and behind it the lush island of Jamaica, dense with its palm and banana trees. She closed her eyes and could almost hear the hypnotic rhythm of steel drums. A mixture of emotions swirled around in her head and chest. Maybe she'd return someday when her life was different. Then she could enjoy all the beauty and warmth the island had to offer. As eager as she was to get home, a part of her already missed this tropical paradise.

And the man who made it so special.

No! She wouldn't think of Jake Alley another second. This whole week had been one giant mistake, beginning with

TJ's infidelity and ending with...with hers? Could that be? Was it just payback time for TJ? She shook her head and retrieved a notepad from her purse. Whatever it was, it was over.

With the end of the pencil poised between her lips, she thought about the week to come, deciding what to write on her list first.

A couple of hours later, over a hot turkey dinner and a large chocolate chip cookie, she went over her notes again, assigning an order and feeling more focused than she had in months.

First, she'd talk with her parents. Tonight. A wave of guilt washed over her thinking of how much hell she'd put them through—what with the wedding and then her sudden disappearance. Somehow she'd make it up to them. And the best way to do that was to show them she was better off without TJ. It'll take time, but they'll see. Her entire life was about to change. Beginning this week.

The flight attendant came and took Catherine's tray, leaving behind the coffee and cookie she was still toying with. Setting the pencil and paper aside, she gave more attention to the cookie, closing her eyes and savoring each tiny morsel. She could never eat a chocolate chip without thinking of Granddad. He always kept her favorite cookies in his desk drawer and made a big production of giving her some whenever she visited him at the store. He'd kept another bag in the limo. An old familiar melancholy sent a shiver up her bare arms. She reached for the blanket on the seat next to her and tucked it around her.

What would Granddad say now if he knew she'd decided to leave Mason's for something so totally foreign. Buying run-down homes and rehabbing them for families in need would sound too liberal for his political persuasion. She snuggled deeper in her blanket, then smiled. He might have called her idealistic, but he'd also say "Go for it, sweetheart." Granddad had always supported her; he would have with this venture, too.

The more she thought about her future, the more excited she became. If only Granddad and his limo were waiting for her when she arrived so she could tell him all her ideas. Catherine closed her eyes and pictured Manny behind the wheel passing her a bag of cookies. She remembered his slow, deep voice warning "Now don't you eat too many, Missy, or you'll get a bellyache and your grandpa will be mighty angry with me."

Her eyes opened wide. How was she getting home from the airport? She hadn't given it a moment's thought, but she needed a ride home. In a flash, she remembered how she got to the airport in the first place. She pictured Jake behind the wheel of his Jeep and just as quickly she turned the image off.

Mom and Dad could probably pick her up, but then she'd run the risk that Jake might try something crazy—like introducing himself. How could she ever explain Jake to them? She barely could explain him to herself. The flight attendant was headed her way and Catherine caught her attention.

"By any chance, do you have a passenger phone?"

"Yes, we do. Would you like to use it?"

"When you get a chance. Please."

A few minutes later she returned with the instrument and Catherine got through on the first try.

"Manny...it's Catherine."

There was a slight pause. "Why, Missy! How are you?" She could hear the smile in his voice but then static sounded in her ear. She decided to get right to the point before she lost the connection.

"Manny, I hate to bother you, but any chance you could pick me up at the airport?"

"You ain't botherin' a thing, Missy. Just watchin' the Tigers lose another game and it's depressin' me somethin' awful. What time your flight arrivin'?"

She got the details out just before the phone crackled and went dead. She leaned back in her seat and exhaled a heavy sigh. Another problem solved. If only the next few days could be so easy.

Suddenly weary, she stowed everything away and slid headphones over her ears, finding an easy-listening station and adjusting the volume to just the right level. With a pillow propped between the window and her seat back, she closed her eyes and leaned against it, surprised when she felt the wheels touch down in Detroit an hour later.

Catherine found Manny at the curb, crisp as ever in his black uniform, leaning cross-armed and cross-ankled against the door of the black stretch limousine. She raced the last few yards to greet him. With one bag in each hand, she threw her arms around the stooped shoulders of the smiling gray-haired man.

"It's so good to see you, Manny," she said over his shoulder, feeling like a little girl again. He patted her back a couple times then gently nudged her away. His crinkled hands shook slightly on her shoulders as he studied her from head to toe.

"Why look at you, Missy...all brown and beautiful." He gave her a wry smile. "A little more sun and you could look like me." He winked and opened the side door and she slid in.

This must be how Dorothy felt when she returned from Oz, Catherine thought, sinking comfortably into the deeply tufted leather seat.

Manny deposited her bags in the trunk, then patiently maneuvered the long vehicle around taxis, buses and throngs of weary travelers while Catherine resumed her thoughts of Granddad.

When he sold Mason's, two binding agreements were part of the deal. One, Manny would remain company chauffeur for as long as he could pass the driving test and when he was ready to retire, he would keep the car. And two, his only grandchild would have a job at Mason's for as long as she chose to work there. Unfortunately there was no stipulation as to what that job might be. Catherine knew that was so she'd have to prove herself, which was fine with her. But sometimes she felt the resentment upstairs.

She sighed and stared through the opened partition. She hoped Granddad wouldn't think she was running away from a challenge. It wasn't that at all. She had many good years at Mason's, but it was time for something new, something that would leave her feeling she made a difference at the end of the day.

Manny made the long, sweeping curve onto Interstate 94 and the traffic thinned. When he looked in his rearview mirror and smiled at her, she pushed away all thoughts of her impending resignation and smiled back.

Over the next few miles, Catherine gave Manny a censored version of her vacation. Then changing the subject abruptly, she asked Manny about his family. Except for his sister, Ellie, who was the only live-in help her parents employed, there were only a couple cousins left in Alabama and he caught her up on their latest doings in a matter of a few sentences.

"Look at that crazy fool." Manny nodded his capped head toward the stake truck in front of them. It was brimming with what looked like scrap metal. "If there was a cop around, he'd get a ticket...driving with an open top like that and all." Manny backed off the accelerator, putting more distance between the two vehicles.

Catherine closed her eyes as a comfortable silence fell over them. The rhythmic sound of the tires rolling over cracks in the concrete lulled her to the edge of sleep. Willingly she drifted along until Manny hit the brakes, jerking her forward.

A big piece of metal was bouncing down the highway straight at them. Manny swerved a hard right. Catherine heard scraping along the underside and she held her breath. The back end fishtailed. Frantically Manny brought the vehicle under control, then pulled onto the wide concrete shoulder and out of the path of traffic. When he stopped he took a big breath and let it out slowly before turning around.

"You okay, Missy?"

She nodded, her stomach still in her throat. "And you?" she asked.

"A little older, if that's possible." He exhaled again. "But I'm fine." He slid to the passenger side and got out to inspect the damage. Catherine followed. The rear tire was slashed and flat, but the rim appeared okay.

"Better get back inside, Missy." Manny placed a protective hand on her shoulder. "Never know when some crazy might run off the road." Reflexively Catherine glanced up the highway.

Manny was right. A crazy was headed right for them.

In a black, topless Jeep.

Catherine ducked into the back seat and shut the door. Through the darkened rear window she saw Jake get out and amble toward Manny. Her heart was pounding. Maybe he didn't see her. Maybe he was just being a Good Samaritan.

The trunk flew up, blocking her vision. She heard their muffled voices along with the clanging of the tire iron and jack being extracted. It sounded as though Jake might change the tire for Manny. For that she was grateful. Manny was getting too old for such things. But why not another passing motorist? Or road service? Why Jake Alley? she wanted to scream.

The men came alongside and Catherine shifted in her seat, facing the opposite way. With any luck, he couldn't see through the dark tinted glass.

Then came the light wrap on the window. She ignored the first one, but a louder, more insistent one followed.

Drat! She reached over and pressed the power switch. The window slid down slowly, Jake's smiling face inches away. He didn't seem surprised to see her. In fact, he seemed to be enjoying her distress.

Again.

What was it with this man? Every time she had a problem, was he going to be there? Her own private guardian devil?

"Having a bit of a problem, *Mrs. Miller?*" He leaned heavily on the name, one corner of his mouth cocked, looking ready to fire another glib remark.

Catherine glared at him, wishing she had a quick comeback, hating herself for the feelings he immediately stirred in her. She'd like nothing better than to say his help wasn't needed and wave him off. But then Manny would insist on changing the tire. If she knew the first thing about it, she'd do it herself. Before she could say anything, his smile disappeared and he made that harrumphing sound of his.

"Well, you just sit back and watch a little TV," he flicked a finger in the direction of the corner set, "or call a few of your friends and tell them all about your vacation." He thumped the top of the car in a dismissing sort of way and then went to work on the tire.

Catherine closed the window, crossed her arms across her chest and fumed. The man was infuriating. Actually she *would* have turned on the TV and watched the end of the baseball game, but after what he'd said, she wouldn't touch the thing. After awhile, however, she did use the phone. She called her parents to let them know they'd be there shortly. Fortunately Ellie answered the phone, which meant she got on and off without explanation.

Finally Manny slid back into the front seat, wiped his brow with a handkerchief, put his cap back on, and then turned to face her. The space between his eyebrows dimpled. "You know that man, Missy?"

She played with a chipped nail and tried to sound nonchalant. "He was on the same plane," she said. Well, that much was true, she thought, as Manny turned around and started the engine. She caught his questioning glance in the rearview mirror just before he pulled out onto the freeway. When she saw Jake's Jeep a few car lengths ahead, she closed her eyes. But it took more than closed eyelids to remove his image from her mind.

Balling her fists in her lap, she forced herself to think of other things. She had more immediate problems to face than that exasperating man. And one of them was just minutes away—her parents.

It wasn't simply facing them tonight that she dreaded. Living under the same roof with them would be the challenge. Since she was supposed to move into TJ's condo after the honeymoon, she'd given up her apartment last month. Mom had thought the few weeks before the wedding would be easier and more fun if her daughter lived at home. Reluctantly Catherine had agreed. Another thing to thank TJ for; the list was growing longer.

She gazed out the window, realizing they were drawing near. Bloomfield Hills, with its massive and regal homes tucked strategically behind manicured acreage, was the most expensive real estate in the Midwest. There were people who would sell their souls—who probably had—to live here. But today, more than any other she could remember, it didn't feel like home. She longed for her cozy little apartment in Birmingham—a place to escape once this night was over.

If they could simply discuss that disastrous night just once and be done with it, things wouldn't be so bad. But she knew Mom. Until Catherine found her own place, Mom would remember one more little tidbit. Then when she tired of that subject, she'd surely want to discuss some lavish party for her fast approaching thirtieth birthday. Then again, after the wedding fiasco Mom might reconsider. A small, intimate affair with just a few guests sounded better to Catherine. That's what she'd suggest when the time came.

She exhaled a loud sigh as the limousine rolled up the long horseshoe driveway off Lone Pine Road and came to a slow stop. With Manny and her bags close behind, she strode up the slate walk to the massive leaded glass and oak doors, squared her shoulders and mumbled under her breath. "Let the games begin."

Nine

Jake stalked into Alley Cat, threw his duffel behind the bar and poured himself a brew, thankful it was Sunday and a slow night. A few regulars were bemoaning the Tigers' latest loss at one end of the bar. Sarge and Tom were at the other end staring at him. Jake finished his mug and poured another before joining them.

He sauntered over and sat on the stool next to Sarge, not in the mood for conversation, but knowing he couldn't escape without a single word.

"Well?" Sarge asked.

Jake slugged back his beer. "Well what?"

"I can see where the vacation improved his disposition, can't you, Tom?"

"Think I'll mosey down to the other end ... see if anybody needs a refill," Tom said, avoiding an answer.

Sarge rolled one wheel and faced Jake. "Want to tell me about it, son?"

Jake finished his beer, wiping his mouth with the back of his hand. "What's to tell? Another beautiful woman ...

another unhappy tale. End of story." He banged his empty mug down on the bar and stood, resting his hand on his father's shoulder. "It's been a long day, Dad. See ya tomorrow."

With that, he pushed through the swinging doors to the kitchen and hiked up the back stairs to his second-floor apartment. For once he was glad his father couldn't follow him. Then he felt like a jerk for thinking such a thought and flopped on the sofa as soon as he let himself in.

He sat in the dark, stale room, the idea of getting up and turning on a light or opening a window seeming too much of an effort. He kicked off his shoes, closed his eyes and tried to doze, but this big black limo kept crossing his screen, replaying and replaying.

The window was lowering in slow motion, inch by inch revealing the black hair he had nuzzled just yesterday morning, the cornflower blue eyes he had gazed into and thought he knew...

He sat up with a start, blinked his eyes and tried to adjust to the dark. The black stretch limo. That's what he should remember and nothing more.

"Humph." He'd been right about her after all. Another spoiled, pampered, self-centered, rich bitch. If he could concentrate on that and not the rest, maybe in time he'd forget her. That little voice was busy at work saying things such as "Who are you kidding?" but he did his best to ignore it.

He staggered into the bedroom and dropped onto the bed, using his last ounce of energy to undress. Why couldn't he just let it go?

The sun filtered through the once-white sheer curtains, its dusty rays settling on Jake's face, nudging him awake. Throwing his legs over the side of the bed with a groan, he stretched and yawned, then stumbled into the bathroom.

A shower and two cups of coffee later, he looked around his shabby apartment with a new attention to detail. Except for last night's clothes left in a heap at the foot of the bed, the apartment was clean and neat, everything in its

place. That's about all he could say nice about it, other than
it was roomy, sprawling over the entire second floor of Alley
Cat.

A few rugs were scattered here and there over the hardwood floor, a floor he'd meant to strip and refinish years
ago, but never did . . . and probably never would. The gray
laminated dinette table with the stainless-steel legs was still
functional, but the cracked red vinyl seats had seen their
better day. The brown threadbare sofa was long and over-
stuffed, dips and mounds in just the right places. There
wasn't a sofa around that could ever feel as right as that one,
Jake thought, refilling his cup.

He drank half the contents, surveying the spacious galley
kitchen with its avocado appliances and worn linoleum
floor. Then he slammed the cup down on the counter, a
slosh of coffee spilling over the rim.

Why did he suddenly care how his digs looked? It wasn't
as though he planned to bring anyone up here. It was just
somewhere to sleep and eat, usually not even that. An image of the limo started to creep to the forefront, but quickly
he pushed it back. A few days of hard work and he'd forget
all about her.

Looking for a distraction, he went to the old oak desk
near the front window and sat down, pulling open a bottom file drawer. He rifled through a pile of dog-eared fold-
ers until he found the one he was looking for. Penciled
across the tab was one word in large printed letters.

Pinstripe.

In Jamaica he'd been able to justify not dealing with Sally's lawyer and the mounting money problems. Everything
was too far away. He puffed out his cheeks, then let the air
escape slowly. Now, there was no excuse. This wasn't going
away.

Last night's exhausting discussion with her parents was
just a warm-up for the challenges Catherine faced at work.

She rode up the escalator, imagining every eye on her,
hearing whispers as she rounded each new corner. There
probably wasn't an employee at Mason's who hadn't heard

about her wedding. But she'd expected this and kept her head high and eyes forward.

It was a little past nine and the store didn't open for another hour. Employees were straightening merchandise on shelves and racks, unpacking new arrivals, counting money in their registers and in general pretending not to see her when she passed. Her walk was brisk, no nonsense, as she approached the executive suite on the third floor.

The new president brought with him a secretary who fancied herself a marine drill sergeant and who ran the office with about as much finesse. Catherine stopped in front of the secretary's desk and waited to be acknowledged, which always took a couple of minutes—control freak that the woman was and especially since Catherine's last name was Mason. The woman was clearly one of those who resented a descendant of the founder working for the company, one who wanted it known Catherine's name carried no weight with her. It was an attitude Catherine guessed her boss shared as well, based on their few conversations.

Eventually the secretary eyed Catherine from above half glasses. "Well, what is it?" she asked and then continued scribbling on her notepad.

"I need to see Mr. Schneider."

"He's busy," she said curtly without looking up again.

"That's okay," Catherine said and started down the hall. "I'll only take a moment of his time."

"Now see here..."

Behind her, she heard the heavy block of a woman huffing around her desk, but Catherine was already at the boss's open door.

He looked up from his paper with a start, then motioned her in. "Come in, Catherine. How was your... I mean... good to have you back," he finally managed with about as much sincerity as a used car salesman. She took a seat in front of him—a leather director's chair, an uncomfortable thing.

Gone was her grandfather's rosewood desk, the oxblood leather chairs and the rows and rows of hard-covered books.

In its place was glass and brass about as warm as the man behind the desk. She decided to get right to the point.

"Mr. Schneider, I'm here to give you my notice."

His eyebrows shot up, but then he quickly recovered and faked a frown. She could imagine him thinking how good it would feel to rid himself of the last Mason. "I see," he said, a hint of condescension creeping into his voice. He began flipping through his planner. There would be no attempt to change her mind, but then she hadn't expected it.

Catherine sat with her hands in her lap, fingers laced, trying to mask her uncertainty. She wasn't a quitter, but this store, these people, even her career choice seemed all wrong. *Yes,* she told herself. She'd made her decision in Jamaica. She wouldn't second-guess herself now.

Schneider closed his book and shrugged. "Would a week from next Friday work for you?"

Catherine felt her pulse quickening. She was actually leaving Granddad's store. She stalled a moment longer, consulting her own calendar, then looked at him squarely. "August 12 will be fine."

He stood and extended his hand. "Good luck, Catherine," he said dismissively.

"Thank you," she said and left his office.

Back at her own desk, she dropped into her chair and stared blindly into space. Everything had gone exactly as she planned. Then why did she feel so lost?

Later that night, when her head finally hit the pillow, her thoughts still tumbled and churned. What would she do with all her spare time after August 12? Inheritance or not, she had to keep busy. She knew what she wanted to do, but how did one get started? After her birthday she'd have all the money she needed, and she already possessed a plethora of ideas, but what did she know about residential construction? If only she had some little project to practice on before she jumped in with both feet. She punched her pillow and rolled over, ignoring what else was bothering her.

But as she drifted off, she heard the lapping of waves and a distant reggae beat . . . and remembered the salty taste of Jake's lips.

* * *

On Wednesday morning, August 10, Jake pushed through the door at the west entrance of Mason's. He hopped onto an escalator and rode to the third floor offices, stopping at the first desk he came to. "Excuse me, is Catherine Mason in?"

The young woman graced him with a toothy smile and said, "Yes, sir, but she's in a meeting."

"That's okay," he said, interrupting her, "I just wanted to leave this for her. Could you see that she gets it?" Jake handed over a sealed envelope.

"Sure," she said, looking first at the blank white envelope then at Jake. "May I tell her who..."

Jake turned and walked away. He told himself he had lucked out not having to see her, but under all the bravado he remembered her sleepy tanned face on the white pillow case just two weeks ago and an ache coursed through him. If he truly wanted to avoid her, why hadn't he mailed the envelope in the first place?

He shook his head. When was he ever going to learn?

Maybe Friday morning's appointment with Pinstripe would knock some sense into his thick skull. He needed a reminder what beautiful women cost him.

By the time Jake got back to Alley Cat he had worked himself into a real snit. In a rush to escape to the privacy of his apartment he didn't notice his friend sitting at the end of the bar until Charlie grabbed his arm.

"Whoa...slow down, cowboy."

Jake jerked his arm free and spun around.

"Charlie! Sorry, man...didn't even see you."

"What's got you in such a state?"

Jake eyed him, then walked behind the bar and poured a draft.

"Jake Alley, if I didn't know you better, I'd think you were havin' woman problems." When Jake shot him a hot glare, Charlie pushed a little further. "Could this mood and your disappearance awhile back have anything to do with that pretty young filly you stole from me last time we crossed paths?"

"She wasn't yours to steal," Jake snapped, instantly wishing he had steered clear of the subject.

"Maybe not, but I dance with her all night, then you up and take off with her."

"I was with her earlier that night." He finished his beer and slammed the mug on the bar. "Let's change the subject, okay?"

Charlie shrugged. "Okay. How 'bout goin' sailin' with me tomorrow?"

"Now you're talkin'."

They made their plan, then settled into safer conversation about Tiger baseball and the upcoming Lion's season. All the while, Jake fought the image of sailing the Caribbean with Catherine. Were even the open waters no longer sacred? Was there nothing he could do, or nowhere he could go, that wouldn't remind him of that impossible woman?

Thursday morning Catherine filled her coffee cup and headed for her desk. She started the day as she did any other—by reading the contents of her in basket. Yesterday, at Schneider's insistence, she'd spent the day screening applicants for her replacement, so now there was a two-day pile of mail. Hurriedly she sorted through the heap, stopping when she came to a plain white envelope. It was sealed with no postage nor even a name on the outside. Curiosity piqued, she tore into it. Inside was a check from Jake. Four words were scribbled in the bottom left corner: *Half of Jamaica expenses.* Pulse racing, she looked inside the envelope hoping for more. Nothing. No note. Zip.

Her first reaction was anger. She wanted to crush the paper into a tiny ball and throw it across the room. But she didn't. There wasn't time for wasted emotion. Not today. She returned the check to the envelope, put it into her purse and went about her business. Not once, for the rest of the afternoon, did she allow herself time to think about Jamaica or the man who gnawed at her subconscience.

By four o'clock, Catherine had made copious notes for her replacement and cleared the last of her personal things from her desk, including TJ's framed portrait, which sat on top of the other trash in her wastebasket. She glanced at the horizontal break in the glass that cut across his jugular. She couldn't have done better if she'd tried. As an afterthought, she retrieved the photo and shoved it into an interoffice envelope. She scribbled Mary Beth's name on the To line, then tossed it in her out basket with an impish smile.

Catherine brushed her hands together in a "that's that" sort of way and looked around the small cubicle. Except for her exit interview with Schneider and the people in personnel tomorrow morning, there was nothing left to do. If this hadn't been Schneider's day off, she could've said her goodbyes today and been out of here. No matter. Tomorrow was a half day. It would be a piece of cake.

At day's end, Catherine stepped outside, a gust of humid air blowing her hair away from her face as she walked to her three-year-old Bonneville. A new car might boost her spirits, she thought idly, merging onto Woodward Avenue. Nothing too ostentatious, though. Besides, she needed something practical if she was going to be haunting construction sites. A Jeep might be fun.

No. Not a Jeep.

She kept her mind occupied with these banal thoughts as she drove away from downtown Birmingham. It wasn't until she reached Twelve Mile Road that she realized she was heading south on Woodward instead of north to her parents'.

Alley Cat was just ahead on the right. She tightened her grip on the wheel. Now how could this be? She'd tuned that man out all day yet here she was a few yards away. She pulled into the parking lot and stared at the entrance. Before she could debate the wisdom of it, she threw open the car door. As long as she was here, she may as well return his check.

She pranced inside thinking he'd probably put up a fuss, but so what? She didn't want his money. She headed directly for the bar where she saw Sarge sitting at the far end. The bartender leaning on the counter talking with him was Tom. Jake was nowhere in sight, a fact that left her slightly rattled.

Sarge's face brightened as she neared him. He rotated one wheel of his chair so that he faced her when she stopped beside him. "Catherine! Good to see you again." He patted the stool in front of him. "Have a seat. I'll buy you a drink."

She was prepared to exchange a few terse words with Jake and be out of here. She hadn't thought about Sarge. But he seemed so genuinely pleased to see her, she found herself sitting down and smiling back.

"You look like you could use a little liquid refreshment. Bad day at the office?"

Tom slid a glass of ice water in front of her and waited on her order. Why not? Just one. "Hectic," she said to Sarge, then turned to Tom. "Bring me a rum and Coke with a twist of lime, please." Suddenly she remembered the only other time she'd had such a drink. Why was she doing this?

Tom returned with her drink and a fresh Coke for Sarge, who lifted his glass and clinked the top of hers.

"Cheers."

"Cheers," she said back, then downed a hefty swallow. The cool room and icy drink felt good. Outside, it was still in the high eighties. Her car's air-conditioning had barely kicked in before she found herself here. She took another swallow, then faced the smiling man next to her.

"So what brings you here, Catherine?"

She'd forgotten about the check. That was the reason she'd come in, wasn't it? Quickly, she rifled through her purse, found the envelope, and handed it to Sarge.

"I wanted to give this to Jake, but it looks like he's not here." She pivoted her stool and glanced around the bar, unsure if she wanted to spot him or not.

"He went sailing with a friend today," Sarge said. She wanted to ask "Male or female?" but couldn't think of a reason to justify her curiosity. Besides, maybe he'd walk in before she finished her drink.

Then Sarge added, "He called a few minutes ago and said it's so nice out they're spending the night on the boat."

Suddenly she felt like crying and didn't know why. What did it matter whether he was with another woman or not?

"You ever sail, Catherine?"

"Once," she said, stirring her drink and staring into it. She should finish this and get out of here. The only reason she was feeling down was that she was tired and tomorrow was her last day at Mason's. That's all.

"Jake rarely takes time off," he said. "I was so glad when he took that vacation."

She stole a sideways glance and saw him grinning from ear to ear. Had Jake told him she was with him? She drank more rum and Coke. Who was she kidding? He'd probably bragged about it to everyone he knew.

"That boy...works far too hard. It's not like he has to, you know."

"Work so many hours, you mean?" Probably to pay for Jamaica, she thought. His ego might be damaged by her returned check, but it sounded as if he could use the money.

"No. I mean work here at all. He doesn't need it."

She swallowed the ice cube in her mouth, nearly choking on it. When she stopped coughing, she swiveled around, the unasked question on her face.

"See that fancy computer against the wall back there," Sarge said, wagging his finger over her shoulder.

She turned and looked, coughed again and nodded her head.

"Well, Jake invented the program that makes it run."

She nodded again, taking a sip of water.

"Never did learn about computers myself. When I started this place—aeons ago—I had a used crank-handle adding machine and a cigar box. That was all I needed."

"*You* started Alley Cat?" Jake had said his parents worked at the bar, not that they owned it. Her head was spinning.

"Didn't Jake tell you?"

She shook her head, wondering what else Jake had left out.

"Well, when I got back from Nam, my sister, Helen, helped me keep things going here. Jake was always good with numbers, so when time came for college he went into computers at Michigan State."

At least that part of the story she knew.

"That's when he designed this bar system. It sold like hot cakes all over the country, and he quit school and bought me out." He snapped his fingers. "Just like that. Came in one day with an old suitcase full of money looking like the cat that swallowed the canary. He knew I wanted to sell but I never had a good offer."

Catherine couldn't believe what she was hearing. The wanna-be cowboy bartender was an inventor? An entrepreneur? Jake Alley? She shook her head at her own stupidity.

Jake Alley. Alley Cat.

How could she have been so dense? Of course. And it was obvious now why he hadn't told her about his success. Sally must have known and look where that got him? Everything was falling into place. Though a little voice warned this shouldn't matter, a louder one said it could make all the difference in the world.

Suddenly she noticed his father was staring at her. She wanted to throw her arms around him and hug his pudgy little neck, but he'd never understand why.

"I'm glad you told me all this, Sarge. Jake is pretty closemouthed about himself. I'm sure you know."

Sarge wasn't smiling anymore. Instead he looked troubled, as if he already regretted what he'd said. She didn't know what to say to make him feel better. Heck, she didn't know what to say to make herself feel better. She felt dizzy and nauseous. One second she was excited with this news; the next embarrassed with the memory of the way she treated Jake their last time together.

She finished her drink and pushed it away, trying to calm herself. This was silly. For all she knew Jake was out on Lake St. Clair with another woman, Jamaica long forgotten—one of many adventures for inventor, entrepreneur, randy Jake Alley. And now, under the close scrutiny of his father, she felt very uneasy. She fumbled for a few bills in her purse but Sarge placed a hand on hers.

"It's on me."

She'd rather pay, but she could see by the look on his face that it wouldn't set well. In fact, she wondered if anything she said right now would set well. He was taking her measure and not being coy about it, either. Did he think she would now go after his son for his money?

This whole situation was laughable but she didn't feel at all like laughing. All she felt like doing was getting out of here and being alone—anyplace where her reactions couldn't be weighed like produce on a scale. She wished she could reassure Sarge his information was safe with her, but without a long explanation, he'd never understand.

She stood and did the best she could with a gentle touch on his shoulder and a wavering smile. "It was good seeing you again, Sarge. I really have to run. Could you ask Jake to call me at the store tomorrow... before noon? Tell him it's very important."

"Sure." He winked and nodded, but the twinkle she'd seen in his eyes when she'd arrived had disappeared. In its place she thought she saw a mixture of anger and mistrust—probably anger with himself for talking too much and mistrust of another woman who suddenly seemed too interested in his son's money.

Catherine walked out wishing she didn't care what his opinion was of her, but knowing for certain that she did.

She got into her car and reminded herself of her resolve to put men on hold until she got her life in order. But she was getting her life in order, she argued with herself. She'd made major strides in the past couple weeks and felt good about her choices.

Was it possible she could have her new life and Jake, too?

She turned the key in the ignition.

Driving away, she tried not to get excited, but with each passing mile the idea took root and grew. By the time she walked up the stairs to her bedroom, it had smothered all other thoughts.

Friday morning Jake thought about going home, showering and putting on decent clothes, but he decided against it. An early-morning swim off Charlie's boat had left him feeling refreshed. Besides, he felt far more comfortable in jeans and a T-shirt. Who was he trying to impress, anyway? Pinstripe wasn't *his* lawyer. He was Sally's.

A block from the downtown Birmingham law office, Jake swung his Jeep into a gas station and stopped alongside a pay phone. He looked at his watch. It was almost ten. Tom would be at the bar taking inventory. He forgot to tell him he'd be late this morning.

Tom answered on the second ring and Jake explained the situation. He was about to hang up when Tom stopped him.

"Sarge wanted to talk to you first thing this morning—before we open."

"Did he say why?"

"No," Tom said, and paused as if something else was on his mind.

"What is it, man? Spit it out."

"Well...that lady friend of yours...the one you were with just before your vacation..."

"Catherine?" What could she have to do with anything?

"Yeah. That was her name. She was here yesterday looking for you."

"Really?" He tried sounding bored.

"It was right after she left that Sarge told me when I talked to you to say he had to see you. Said it was important."

Now what could this be all about? "Tell him I'll be there as soon as I can. Thanks, Tom." He hung up and merged onto Hunter Boulevard trying to puzzle it out.

A few minutes later he parked his Jeep and strode into the attorney's office, still distracted by Tom's message. When the secretary ushered him back to Pinstripe's office and Jake saw the smug smile on the little twerp's face, he forgot all about Catherine.

Catherine walked out of Schneider's office and stopped to look at her watch. It was eleven forty-five. There was time to float around and say a few goodbyes, but she'd already seen everyone who mattered. She was free to go. She'd just check her desk for messages first.

In case anyone called.

Like Jake.

She rounded the corner, heart pounding, hoping to find a pink While You Were Away message lying on her desk. The top was bare. She blew out the breath she hadn't realized she'd been holding. Why was she doing this to herself? If he had any intention of calling her, he would've done so by now.

But in the event she was wrong, she stopped at the reception desk on her way to the rest room and left word to be paged if a Jake Alley should happen to call. She walked on, glancing at her watch again. He had ten minutes. If he didn't call by then, she'd write him off as a lost cause. Somehow, once and for all, she'd have to bury the fantasies that had kept her awake all night.

Hair freshly brushed and lipstick reapplied, she left the ladies' room and walked slowly to the escalator, still listening for a page. She rode to the first floor, feeling numb, already a stranger in a place she'd spent half her life. No longer did the crystal chandeliers nor massive floral arrangements hold any magic.

When she pushed through the revolving door and stepped outside, she knew two chapters in her life had just ended. Driving away she watched the Birmingham store slowly disappear from sight. But the tug on her heartstrings she'd expected wasn't there. Leaving her grandfather's store wasn't the finale that hurt the most.

On the way to Alley Cat, Jake tried to remember who it was that said "First, we kill all the lawyers." Whoever he was, he was a man to be admired.

Jake had tried his best to be civil to Pinstripe, but there wasn't any blood in those icy veins. If he had cut one open, which he had felt like doing more than once, he was sure green cubes with dollar signs would've spewed out.

As calmly as possible, Jake had explained he'd saved half the money owed Sally, but it was unlikely he could come up with the whole amount by the deadline.

Pinstripe steepled his fingers and rocked back, smiling his unctuous smile.

"I'm sorry, Mr. Alley, but the settlement clearly states that either you pay my client half the value of the business by November 1, or you hand over the keys to Alley Cat." He must have been crazy when he signed that property settlement, but his own attorney had said he had no choice.

"Actually my client was very generous in giving you five years to pay," Pinstripe added, still smiling. Jake wondered how much it would cost if he shoved the jerk's teeth down his throat. Still, he kept his cool and even offered to hand over all the money he had now, if only she'd extend the payoff time a little longer.

"Now why would we do that, Mr. Alley? When we could have the whole thing November 1."

What was that *we* crap? Jake wondered, pulling up behind the bar. How much was Sally forking over to that creep, anyway?

When Jake opened the front door and saw his father reading the paper in his usual spot, he decided to shelf the Sally problem. It needed more thought but now wasn't the time. Right now he wanted to hear what Sarge had to say that was so almighty urgent. If his gut was right, it had something to with Ms. Mason. And that could mean only one thing.

Trouble.

It only took a couple of sentences from his father to prove he'd been right.

"You told her *what?*" Jake shouted. The lunch crowd around him grew still. Quickly he unlocked his father's chair and wheeled him past the swinging doors and out through the kitchen, not stopping until they were down the ramp and outside, flanked by a pair of rusty garbage bins.

"I assumed she knew most of it already. She was with you on vacation, wasn't she?"

They hadn't discussed it, but he knew his father had figured it out from the get-go. "Whether she was or wasn't has nothing to do with this discussion."

"Well, sure it does. I figured if she talked you into a vacation and you spent a week with her, she must be someone special."

His father would never understand, even if Jake tried to explain, which he couldn't since the whole thing was a big pile of mush in his own mind. He let out a long sigh and pressed his back against the block wall.

Okay, so she knew he owned the place. And she knew he sold some software, though that source of income had dried up once newer systems came on the market—a fact he'd withheld from his father, like all his other money problems. Jake crossed his arms. Why was he making such a big deal out of this? It wasn't as if he planned to see the woman again.

"I'm sorry, Jake." His father's sad eyes begged for forgiveness. "I know how much you guard your privacy and I can't say as I blame you." He stared off, looking as though his own past should have taught him not to trust women.

"It's okay, Dad. I'm sorry, too." Jake kicked some gravel, then decided to explain his foul mood. "I just came from Sally's attorney. Guess you got the hot air I should have blown at him."

"Problem?"

"Nothing I can't work out." Jake smiled and grabbed the handles of the chair. "Come on. Let's go back inside where it's cooler. I'll buy ya lunch."

He'd spared his father the details of the divorce at the time. He wasn't about to burden him with it now. Besides, he *would* work it out. There was no way Sally would get her hands on Alley Cat. She'd already gotten his boat—a fact that stuck in his craw all these years later.

After a quick bowl of chili and a neutral exchange of baseball news, Jake left Sarge with his paper and wandered upstairs, clutching Catherine's envelope.

It was past noon, but he decided to call her anyway. If she was out to lunch, all the better. He'd leave a message saying to expect the delivery of a "nonreturnable package." And then that would be that. But he wasn't prepared for the response he got from the gruff, middle-aged woman on the other end of the line.

"What do you mean she doesn't work there anymore?" Jake asked.

"Exactly that," came the terse reply. "She quit. Left around noon."

Catherine had told him in Jamaica she planned to quit, but he couldn't believe she actually left the family store. Worse yet, he didn't like the way the news punched him in the gut. Had she left town, too?

"Could you give me her address? I have something to send her."

"We can't give out that information. You could send it here and we'll forward it." Without waiting for a reply, the line went dead.

Fingers trembling, Jake found a fresh envelope, addressed it and inserted the check. As an afterthought he scribbled a short note.

Catherine,
A deal's a deal, so here's your check back. Good luck on your new job or whatever you're up to. If you're ever thirsty and feel like slumming it again, stop by and I'll buy you a drink.

Jake

Before he could dwell on the wisdom of his words, he stuffed the paper inside and licked the flap. It was over. She was gone. No use making an enemy out of the woman. Besides, he didn't have to worry about her taking him up on the offer. He'd bet his boots he'd never lay eyes on her again. The question was—why did that make him feel as if he'd just wallowed barefoot through a muddy cow pasture?

Ten

Three weeks passed and Catherine still found herself idle. She sat under an umbrella table near the pool, sipping orange juice and ignoring the *Detroit News* classifieds on her lap. Her mother sat across from her nibbling dry toast.

"Where did you go, Catherine?" she asked, toast poised midair.

Catherine blinked then looked at her mother. "I was just thinking about—about my future." And Jake.

Her mother wiped her mouth with a napkin. "We've been so busy I haven't given it much thought—how much you must miss Mason's."

"That's not really it, Mom. I'm not sorry I left. I'm just impatient to move on to the next phase of my life—if only I could decide where to begin." She pushed her plate away, no longer hungry.

"Improving neighborhoods and providing homes for those in need is certainly an ambitious goal."

Catherine glanced at her mother, looking for signs of disapproval, finding none.

"Ever since you told us about your plans, I've been thinking about this organization one of my groups raises funds for. It's called *Habitat for Humanity*. Have you ever heard of it?"

"I remember you and some of your friends discussing it over bridge, but I don't remember any details."

"Let me tell you how it works." Mom propped her elbows on the table and excitedly poured out what she knew. Families in need of a home would work side by side with volunteers and skilled tradespeople. When the project was finished, *Habitat* would sell the home at cost, financing it themselves, to the family who worked it.

"That's where we come in," Mom concluded. "We help raise mortgage money. But I know they're always looking for workers. Not just tradespeople, but organizers, coordinators, all kinds of volunteers."

Catherine sat quietly and took it all in. It sounded like just the group she needed. She wished she could show more enthusiasm for her mother's idea, but right now something else was crowding her thoughts.

After a few silent minutes, her mother changed subjects.

"Are you sure you don't want to go to Traverse City with us this weekend. There's plenty of room at the condo and your father won't be ready to leave for another hour."

"Thanks, Mom, but no." The house to herself for the long Labor Day weekend sounded...sounded...she wanted to say peaceful, but the word that came to mind was lonely.

Finally her mother leaned closer and whispered, "Come on, Catherine. What's this really about?"

"I got a letter in the mail yesterday from Dad's attorney...reiterating the fact I'm a free woman. He had TJ sign off on everything so there won't be any legal challenge down the road. Guess I'm feeling a little sorry for myself," she said, hoping this would put an end to the discussion. But it didn't.

"I thought you said it was for the best—that marrying TJ was the biggest mistake of your life."

Catherine emptied her glass and shifted her gaze to the pool. "I still feel that way. The letter just reminded me what a fool I was, that's all." If only they could talk about Jake and what was really bothering her. But her mother would never understand. It was hard enough to explain it to herself. She stared at a lone red leaf floating on the clear blue water.

"Dear, why don't you put closure to this thing—whatever it is you're not telling me—once and for all." Surprised, Catherine glanced at her wise mother, then quickly away. "We'll leave a number where we can be reached. Call me if you need anything—even if it's just to talk to a worrywart old mother." She touched Catherine's shoulder then sauntered inside.

Catherine sat stunned and silent, her heart in her throat, her mother's words echoing in her head: *Why don't you put closure to this thing—once and for all.*

He did invite her to stop in for a drink when he mailed the check back....

Catherine went over and over it in her head on the drive down Woodward. She'd stroll in casually. If Sarge was there, she'd sit next to him and do a little fence-mending. Being a holiday and a Friday night, Jake would probably be busy. It could take awhile before he had time to visit with her. While she waited she'd observe him from afar. Maybe he'd flirt with an overly made-up floozy at the bar and ignore her. Maybe she wouldn't even like his looks anymore. He could've grown a beard or gotten a brush cut as far as she knew. Or sampled too much of his own brew and developed a beer belly. Or taken up the habit of snacking on raw garlic.

But if she believed any of that—or thought it mattered—she wouldn't be here.

She parked outside Alley Cat and a wave of déjà vu crept over her. Before she could change her mind she headed for the door. Self-conscious of how it may appear walking into the bar alone—again—she hesitated at the door. Finally she flung it open and strode in. The familiar sound of country twang and boot stomping greeted her and an eerie feeling flooded her senses.

It felt like coming home.

She didn't move for the longest moment, taking it all in, stunned by the feeling of pleasure this place gave her. On the crowded dance floor, line dancers of all ages, shapes and colors were stepping and turning in unison. Others were slugging back beer from the bottle and singing along.

"Catherine!" A towering, hard body crushed against her in a bear hug and she staggered a step backward. When he released her she looked up into the familiar smiling face.

"Charlie," she laughed. "It's good to see you, too."

"Gosh, it's been ages, beautiful." He tugged on her arm, pulling her toward the bar.

Sarge was working on a plate of nachos and didn't see them coming. When he eventually looked up, there was the old happy twinkle in his eyes that she'd remembered. He wiped his mouth hastily with a paper napkin and extended both arms to her. She bent to kiss him on the cheek as he thumped her back with gusto. When he emptied his mouth, he squeezed her hand and smiled in a way that said their last conversation was all but forgotten. "You're the last person I expected to see here tonight. What a wonderful surprise."

Charlie pulled out a pair of stools. "She probably had to come back here to find some real men," he said, winking at Catherine.

Another time she might have come up with a clever retort, but for now she let it slide. She liked this cowboy. She half listened to the pair as her gaze trailed cautiously down the long bar. Tom was at the far end drying glasses and visiting with a couple of patrons.

No one else was behind the counter.

Suddenly the disappointment was so acute, she felt a lump pushing at the back of her throat. If she'd been able to kid herself before, she couldn't now. She wanted to see Jake.

Tonight.

Badly.

She lowered her eyes and fumbled for a tissue in her purse, grateful that the music and crowd had grown louder making conversation nearly impossible. Chin on her chest she began lecturing herself on the foolishness of this impulsive visit. It'd been a mistake to assume he'd be here. A big-ger mistake to let herself think he'd care if he ever saw her again.

Catherine blew her nose and then straightened her shoulders. As long as she was here she may as well have a drink. Whenever Tom made his way down to this end she'd order...

A Baileys on the rocks slid slowly on the counter in front of her. Long, tanned fingers rested patiently on the napkin beneath it, instantly stirring an old familiar longing—first in her chest, then quickly spreading to other parts. She stared at his hand wishing he'd speak, sensing he wouldn't. Slowly she let her gaze travel up the long, sinewy arms in rolled white shirtsleeves, to the broad shoulders, stopping on the exposed thatch of golden hair above the top button. There she lingered, steeling herself for the final piece of the puzzle.

What would she find in his eyes? Love? Hate? Or worse—indifference. Releasing the breath she'd been holding she looked for her answer.

And found none.

His pupils were nearly black. They said nothing but asked everything. She searched his face hoping for a clue as to how he felt but his features were a mask, patiently waiting for her to make the first move. Almost on cue the band stopped playing. The silence, and Jake's close scrutiny, were more than she could bear. The corners of her mouth tugged upward and she gave in.

"How did you know I'd like Baileys?" She watched him exhale.

"When you've done this job for as long as I have, you learn."

She leaned in closer and flashed him a coy smile, hoping she'd broken through his glacial facade. "What else have you learned in all that time?"

He met her gaze evenly. "The difference between when a lady stops in for a drink and when she wants something more."

Catherine felt the heat creep up her neck. She glanced over her shoulder and wasn't surprised to find Sarge and Charlie openly staring. She turned back to the bar and stirred her Baileys, wishing there was a hole she could crawl into, when Jake came around the end of the bar and grabbed her hand.

"Come on, let's get out of here." Before she could object he called to a passing waitress. "Trudy... work the bar for a while, will ya?"

Trudy gave Catherine the once-over, then smiled and said, "Sure thing, boss. Take your time."

Jake stalked through the kitchen and out the back door, Catherine in tow, all without a word. It was too late to argue with him. The feel of his warm hand on hers had made her accept the truth. She knew how she felt about this man. Now it was time she found out how he felt about her. Good or bad. She had to know.

He spun around to face her, his nose inches from hers.

"Okay, Mrs. Miller. Enough of your cute little word games."

In spite of her intentions, she bristled at his approach. "I'm not Mrs. Miller. I told you before it wasn't legal." She thought she saw something in his eyes but he didn't change his tone.

"That's beside the point. Why are you here? And don't say I invited you to stop in for a drink, because we both know there's more to this little visit."

He wasn't making this easy, but he was right. Still, she wasn't going to discuss this nose to nose, watching him grate his teeth. She turned her back to him and started hesitantly. "The day before I left Mason's, I stopped by to see you..."

"Yes, yes. I know that," he said, interrupting her.

She took a deep breath and exhaled slowly. He was making her angry.

"For God's sake, Catherine. Spit it out."

"I stopped by to see you because I hoped you would... that you would say you..." Her voice broke and she felt her chin begin to quiver. *Damn.* She wasn't going to cry. Clenching her fists she pushed on. "That you were glad to see me." And more, damn it. So much more.

Instead of the response she'd hoped for, she heard nothing. Confused, she kept talking. "I left a message with Sarge for you to call me before I left Mason's, but you never did."

"I called you that day," he said softly to her back.

She turned around. "When?" There was a softness around his eyes now, but still he didn't touch her.

"They said I just missed you. You'd already left."

More than anything, she wanted him to hold her. She tried to convey this with a look but it didn't work. He stood there, arms folded, staring at her as though he were trying to read her true motives for being there—as if she had come for some diabolical reason.

"Did your father tell you we talked?" The words were no sooner out than she saw him stiffen. Suddenly she thought she knew what was wrong. "Look, just because I know you own this place—" she pointed angrily to the building beside them "—is no reason to get so damnably defensive." Frustration at his bullheadedness was quickly replacing hurt. "I don't need your money, if that's what you're thinking."

"No, probably not," he said with a sneer. "Daddy has plenty."

"Yes, he does." She stepped in closer, nose to nose as he'd done to her before. "But I have more. Much more." She hadn't meant for him to know yet. Certainly not this way. But now it was out.

"Right. An unemployed department store buyer makes more money than a Bloomfield Hills broker. Try again, Catherine."

She exhaled a hot breath right in his face and spoke again between clenched teeth. "Okay, Mr. Know-It-All. On my thirtieth birthday, I stand to inherit the bulk of my grandfather's estate, which I think I'm safe in saying is a tidy sum larger than yours and my parents combined net worth." Her hands rose to her hips as she inched closer to his unreadable face. "So what do you have to say to that?"

"When's your thirtieth birthday?" he asked, completely deadpan.

"October 8," she answered suspiciously. "What else do you want to know?"

"Why you waited so long to come see me?"

"You...you, egotistical, self-righteous jackass!" She pounded on his chest with both fists. When she tried to back away he grabbed her wrists and held her tight.

"Well? Are you glad to see me?" he asked.

"Are you?" she asked back.

"I asked first." A hint of a smile tugged at one corner of his mouth.

She stared into his eyes already knowing his answer, never doubting for a second her own.

"Yes," she whispered softly, her gaze not leaving his.

"Yes," he whispered back, then gently kissed the single tear that streaked down her face. He pulled her closer, stroking her hair as she pressed her damp cheek to his chest.

Catherine wrapped her arms around his waist and held on, afraid if she opened her eyes it would all disappear like a dream.

"God you feel good, Cat," he said into her hair.

He rubbed her back and squeezed her tighter, in a way that said what she felt—they could never be too close. Eventually he pulled away and looked down at her with eyes she hadn't seen since Jamaica. Without a word he took her hand and led her up the fire escape to his apartment, to the place she'd wanted to go from the moment she'd laid eyes on him.

Jake awoke first, uncertain if he'd ever slept. The window air conditioner hummed away, barely keeping up with the Labor Day weekend heat wave.

He looked around his drab and sparsely furnished apartment, wondering again what Catherine thought of his shabby digs. He knew she'd say it didn't matter. But it did to him. He wanted her with him always, but how could she live in a dump like this?

He threw his legs over the side of the bed and looked over his shoulder, still not believing she was beside him. And had been all night. She was on her side, her back to him, sound asleep.

Gently he lifted off the mattress and padded naked to the kitchen. He made a pot of coffee and waited for it to drip through, suddenly angry with Sally and her greedy attorney. If it weren't for all the money they were sucking out of him, he could afford a real home for Cat and himself. Now what did he have to offer her? And if she knew he was in hock up to his eyebrows, what then?

It was hard to think. Not only was he sleep deprived, but all the blood had left his brain. He looked down and shook his head in amazement. That gal was going to be the death of him yet.

The coffee was ready. He poured two cups, found a tray and carried it back to bed. Catherine rolled over and pulled the sheet modestly to her chest.

"Ummm." She sniffed deeply without opening her eyes. "Is that coffee I smell?"

"It's all I had time to make."

She opened one eye and then giggled.

"Hardly." She extended one arm to him. "Put the tray down and come here, you sexy devil."

"My, but you're bossy," he said, but did as he was told.

When he buried his face in the crook of her neck she said, "Get used to it."

"I guess there's only one way I can shut you up." He captured her mouth.

Into it she mumbled, "Uh-huh."

He couldn't believe he wanted her again. They'd been in bed for over eight hours. But all this closeness did was leave him wanting more.

He nibbled at her breast and listened to her moan with delight, her body writhing below him, rising to meet his. She was just as hungry for him and didn't try to hide it, a thought that both excited and challenged him to new heights. He wanted to please her, each time bringing her to a higher plateau. His gaze held hers for a tender moment, then she began to cry. Startled, he pulled her into his arms.

"Cat, Cat . . . what is it?"

She shook her head but cried harder. He held her tight and rocked with her, letting her tears run their course. When they had, he handed her a tissue and she gave a good blow. He stroked her hair and waited.

Finally she looked up at him sheepishly.

"What's wrong?" he asked, not having a clue.

"Nothing's wrong. It's just that I'm so happyyy..." Then she started again.

"Women!" he said with a chuckle, and handed her the whole box of tissues. She dabbed at her face and then buried it in his chest. The next thing he knew she was giggling again. Go figure.

He lifted her chin then leaped from the bed. "Breakfast time. You know how to cook?"

Catherine played with the sheet and didn't meet his gaze.

"Just as I thought." He reached out for her hand and tugged her to her feet. "Come on. We'll make breakfast together. It's about time you learn."

Jake pulled on his jeans that lay abandoned on the floor from last night and Catherine slipped on his white shirt, nuzzling the collar to her nose and smiling.

A few broken eggs and burnt toast later they sat down to breakfast. It didn't matter how it tasted. They were both famished.

Jake refilled their coffee mugs and listened to Catherine's plans for *Habitat,* all the while picturing her in a hard hat and tool belt and nothing else. This woman was full of surprises. Trading designer clothes for jeans and work boots. Not that she actually had to do any hard labor, but he already knew she would.

Catherine rubbed her toast around the rim of her egg-covered plate before she polished off the last crust. Out of story as well as food, she finally licked her fingers one at a time.

Jake smiled. Somehow he couldn't see her doing that at home. Of course he couldn't imagine her doing any of the other things she'd done since she walked up those back steps, either.

"What?" she asked.

"What do you mean 'what'?" His smile widened.

"What are you grinning at?"

"Just you...cleaning your plate, smacking your fingers."

"What's so amusing about that?"

"Bet you don't eat that way with Mommy and Daddy."

"Bet you'll find out next month." She downed her coffee looking smug, then walked to the kitchen for the pot. He lifted his mug and she poured.

"I'm afraid to ask...."

"You don't have to come to my birthday party." She smiled confidently. "But it's a big deal to my parents and I promised I'd be there."

"I suppose that means a suit."

"Yep." She slurped her hot coffee and giggled, he thought more from her atypical behavior than the idea of him tugging at a dreaded tie or meeting her parents.

For the first time this morning Jake looked at his watch and swore. It was after ten. He was expected downstairs in less than an hour. It was bad enough he'd skipped out early last night, he wasn't covered for lunch. He had to go.

They worked out a plan. He'd go to work while Catherine took her time showering and dressing. She'd go home for some fresh clothes and an overnight bag and meet him back here at six.

Jake showered and dressed quickly and was about to go downstairs. He checked the time again. It was twenty to eleven. He was actually ahead of schedule. Or so he thought...until he kissed her goodbye. Then he was five minutes late.

Catherine had time to kill. She cleaned up the kitchen, then strolled leisurely around the sprawling apartment. If she couldn't be with Jake right now, this was the next best thing. It seemed so personal somehow, being among his things, his private world.

She made the bed then dropped on top of it and lay with her hands locked behind her head. The ceiling was at least ten feet with the exposed mechanicals painted a soft blue-gray. The windows had little wooden panes that seemed in good shape. The hardwood floor could use refinishing but the wood was intact, no missing or broken boards. This place had all kinds of interesting possibilities.

An eerie feeling crept over her. For some reason she didn't think she would ever live here. Not that she couldn't or wouldn't. Not even because Jake hadn't asked her yet. She knew it was just a matter of time. It was something else. She tried to put a finger on it, but each new thought ended with the same question—How could her money not create a problem with an independent man like Jake?

Frustrated, she bounded out of bed and headed for the shower. She was in love. For now, she'd enjoy that much and worry about the rest later. Somehow, she and Jake would find a way to be together.

They had burgers and fries at the bar when Catherine returned, then ogled each other from across the counter, sneaking up the back stairs during breaks for hot, passionate kisses. Catherine felt like a teenager up to no good and she loved every minute of it.

At midnight, when Tim and Tom had things under control behind the bar, Jake grabbed Catherine's hand for one last trip up the stairs. Once behind closed doors, he popped the cork on a bottle of Chablis and dropped heavily beside Catherine. They sat on the sofa and toasted each other with silly little sentiments, laughing and kissing and getting a little buzz.

Catherine extended her glass in front of her for a refill, feeling as though she would burst with happiness. So this was what love was all about, she thought. With TJ, it had felt comfortable. Inevitable, actually. But with Jake she felt so excited she thought if she stood and held out her arms she might actually fly away. Her emotions were so intense, she could do little but sit there and let them dance through her veins. How could she ever give back to this man half as much as he had already given her?

She watched him as he walked to the kitchen and disposed of the empty bottle. While he filled a couple of glasses with ice water, she thought again about her inheritance. It would be tricky spending any of it on this proud man. She'd have to tread lightly. But surely there had to be a way to share it with him.

Jake returned and handed her the water. She drank half of it before she spoke.

"Tell me something, Jake." She cocked her head and eyed him coyly. "If you won the lottery—"

"I don't even buy tickets." He interrupted her.

"Come on, play along a minute." She trailed her fingers up his arm. He bent his head and kissed the hollow of her collarbone. She hunched her shoulder, nudging him away.

"Okay. We'll play your little game . . . first." The playful twinkle in his eyes made it clear he had other ideas.

"So, you just won the lottery." She inched back a little. "And you knew that I always wanted a red Porsche. What would you do?"

"Try to talk you into a green Jag. I like them better." She punched at his shoulder. "But if I couldn't, I'd buy you your red Porsche." He tried pulling her back to him but she locked her elbows and pressed firmly against his chest.

"And if I said we'd just have to live on what I made—if I ever get a job—" She rolled her eyes. "Or if I said I couldn't accept such an expensive gift, would you get angry with me?"

"I'd throw you over my knee and spank your cute little butt."

"Seriously."

He eyed her suspiciously. "What's this all about, Cat? You're not thinking of buying me a car? If you are, forget it, I . . ."

She laughed and tossed her hair from side to side. "No, I'm not thinking of buying you a car."

"Then what? What's this all about?"

She averted her eyes. "Oh, nothing." She knew he didn't believe her. She tried again. "It's nothing. Really. I was thinking of buying myself a new car and wondered what kind you liked." She looked up into his eyes and flashed him her most sincere smile. "Relax, smarty-pants, I'm not going to replace your glorious Jeep. It holds too many fond memories." She pushed him and he fell willingly onto the cushions. "But I am going to give you something else you want."

"Yes, you are," he said, pulling her toward him. "Right now."

She felt his warm lips press against hers and she swallowed a chuckle. She couldn't care less about a new car—for herself or for him. There was something else she knew Jake wanted and she would get it for him, regardless of the cost.

But for now, as he kissed his way down her neck, she let him assume he knew exactly what was on her mind.

Monday night Jake stood in the parking lot and waved until Cat's taillights vanished from view. Her perfume lingered on his shirt and he felt more alone than he could ever remember. After sharing the same room in Jamaica, it had felt strange not seeing her, even though he'd convinced himself it was for the best. But now? Now there was no denying how they both felt. And it hurt like hell to see her carry her suitcase out his door.

At last he turned and stared at Alley Cat. For the first time in his life he resented the business that had been his life. It was just a pile of bricks and mortar. Nothing compared to Catherine. And she deserved so much better than living over a bar. He looked up at the neon sign. How long would it be before she tired of this place? Or of him?

Sad and weary, he trudged up the back stairs and let himself in. It was dusk and dark shadows danced across the wooden floor. He stretched out on the lumpy sofa and closed his eyes, not bothering to turn on a light. The phone rang in the kitchen. Someone downstairs must have heard him come in. He was due behind the bar a half hour ago. It rang a second time. Then a third.

Finally he swore and stumbled to the kitchen. "Hello?"
There was static on the other end. "I miss you, cowboy."
"Cat?"

"Is there another woman you were expecting to hear from?"

Compared to the sad face he'd seen when she left, he was glad to hear the smile back in her voice. "I didn't expect to hear from you tonight." He laughed, a mixture of nerves and excitement.

"I don't know about you, Jake Alley. You have strange powers over me."

"You rich ladies and your car phones," he teased. "Is that what you couldn't wait to tell me?"

"No, it isn't, Mr. Know-It-All."

Out of the blue he told her what he was thinking before the phone rang. "I wish I could afford to buy you a house, Cat. I can't see you ever living in this dump." The words were no sooner out of his mouth than he realized they'd never talked about living together. He knew she wanted to be with him, but the big *M* had yet to be mentioned.

"Jake Alley, you better get hold of yourself. If you think where I live matters, you're crazier than I thought you were. It only matters that we're together."

He breathed a sigh of relief. There was more static and for a moment he thought they'd lost the connection, but then he heard her.

"But now that you mention it, I did have an idea if you're ready to hear it."

"Shoot. It's your money."

"See. Having a few bucks isn't so bad, is it?"

"So... you going to tell me this idea or keep me in suspense all night."

"Well, I was just remembering you said something about remodeling the downstairs yourself. You know I want to work with *Habitat,* but I could use a little practice first."

"Yes?" Now, what was she up to?

"What if I put up the downpayment and together we fix up a house. It doesn't have to be big or fancy. There are lots of fixer-uppers in Birmingham or Royal Oak. Later we could either sell the place or move in, depending on whether we're still speaking.''

The only thing keeping him from saying yes was his male ego. Besides, he liked the idea. "We could start looking tomorrow. Is that soon enough?''

"Have I told you how crazy I am about you, cowboy?''

"Not since you abandoned me in the parking lot ten minutes ago.''

She ignored his jab. "Maybe we should take a camera.''

"There's one in my Jeep.''

"Speaking of photos, could you take a few more for me?''

"I'm afraid to ask. What of?''

She hesitated, then gave him the short version. "Of your apartment. I had another idea but I'll need some pictures first. A floor plan or old blueprints would be helpful, too.''

"I'm confused. If we find a house, why mess with this place?''

She hesitated a moment, then said, "Let's talk about it later, maybe tomorrow when I see you.''

"I'll be here with bells on." He laughed and added, "Doesn't that conjure up an interesting image?''

"You're just a dirty old man, you know that?''

"Nah. I'm not so old.''

Jake turned on a light, flopped back onto the sofa and cupped his hands behind his head. He stared at the chipped ceiling overhead. What was she up to now? And why did he still have this hang-up about her money? She had it to burn... or would soon. If only he weren't scraping the bottom of the barrel.

He braced his elbows on his knees and supported his cheeks in his palms. There was a dirty spot on the throw rug under his feet. He thought about washing it. Anything sounded better than worrying about Sally and Pinstripe.

How in the hell was he going to come up with that much money?

He slapped his thighs and staggered to the bedroom. All he had to do was ask Catherine and she'd give him the money in a flash. But could he live with himself if he took it? Besides, she didn't even know there was a debt to be paid and that's the way he was going to keep it. Somehow, he'd find a way to pay off Sally. Then, and only then, would he ask Cat to be his wife.

A couple of weeks of house hunting and they were still speaking to each other. Amazing, Jake thought. They sat at the corner booth of Toot's Diner and ate breakfast in silence. Jake looked at Cat from time to time as she scanned the classifieds.

This wasn't at all how he'd envisioned love. In truth, all he'd pictured was the two of them in bed, barely leaving the room or coming up for air. What surprised him was what a small part that played in his newfound happiness.

He drained his orange juice glass, then eyed her in wonder. Yes, he'd enjoyed the feeling of being inside her earlier this morning. But for the first time in his life, at this very moment, he knew what it was like to feel a woman inside of him. She had found the spot. No, he corrected himself. She had filled the void he hadn't even realized was there. If he hadn't known it before, he knew it now. He loved this woman in a way he didn't think possible, and with such intensity that at the moment it hurt.

Sometime during his haze, Catherine had spoken. It took a moment for him to focus on her words.

"Jake?" She reached out and touched his hand, the simple gesture magnifying his feelings. "Did you bring the pictures?"

"The pictures." He nodded. "Yes, of course. I brought lots of pictures." He rifled through a canvas bag and retrieved them, along with the requested blueprints of Alley Cat. Waving the long roll in front of her, he said, "I brought these, too... but you still haven't told me why."

Catherine pushed their dishes aside and reached for the photos. "All in due time, my love. First, show me our new house."

Jake gave her one set at a time. *Our* house, he thought. It was no longer *the* house. The transition had been smooth and mutual. He handed her the last set of photos, his favorite.

"Oh, Jake. I love this one. Bay windows, hardwood floors and trim. How many bedrooms did it have?"

"Master downstairs and three up. Plenty of room for..." Lots of kids, he'd almost said, but caught himself in time. They hadn't even talked about marriage, let alone children. But watching Cat's face told him all he wanted to know.

"One of the upstairs bedrooms has a skylight," he continued. "It would make a perfect at-home office, if you thought you'd like something like that."

She looked up from the photo in her hand, her face telling him she hadn't missed the topic he'd so carefully skirted. There was a flicker of a shy smile.

"Do you like this one?" she asked, holding his steady gaze.

"Yes, I do," he said.

The light in her eyes brightened. "Let's buy it."

"Don't you want to see more?"

She waved the top photo. "Nope. It's perfect." She stood the pile of pictures on their sides and tapped them into order like a deck of cards, then set them aside.

"Now...do you want to hear my idea for Alley Cat?" She reached for the prints and spread them open between them. "Oh, yes," she said excitedly, looking suddenly like a child at Christmas. "Jake, it will work. I just feel it in my bones."

She'd stolen his heart, but his business was something else. Alley Cat was all he had—the only thing he could call his own. As silly or selfish as it might seem, he wasn't sure he wanted to share it. He certainly didn't want ruffled curtains and matching seat covers. Or worse yet, a clutter of antiques. Yet, he reminded himself, not long ago he thought of it as just a pile of bricks.

He folded his arms and leaned back, eyeing her suspiciously from the side of his face. "Okay, whatcha got in mind?"

She opened her briefcase on the seat beside her, hesitated, then handed over a stack of sketches and notes. He started to read the top page when she stopped him.

"No. Not now. I know you have to get to work. Take them with you. When you're ready, let me know what you think."

Jake breathed a sigh of relief. They hadn't had a harsh word since their reunion. But this might be treading on dangerous ground.

He looked at his watch, grateful for a change that it was time for work.

"Good idea," he said, grabbing the check and standing.

"Think I'll stay here and finish the paper," she said.

Jake brushed her cheek with a light kiss and left.

Through the window, Catherine watched the Jeep leave the parking lot and her eyes blurred over. God, how she loved that man. But were they moving too fast? Did she know everything about him she should? She thought she'd known TJ. Look how wrong she'd been then.

She drank the last of her coffee and asked herself a more difficult question. Why hadn't Jake mentioned marriage? Not once. True, it hadn't been long since their reunion, but there was no doubt they would be together, that an unspoken commitment had been made.

So, was it his bad experience with Sally? Or her own disastrous trip down the aisle last July? Did he think she'd say no? Or didn't he want the formality of marriage?

She folded the paper and put it in her briefcase, then stared out the window, realizing the true source of angst. Her granddad's words echoed in her head as clear as if he'd been sitting across from her. *Love alone is not enough...he must have money of his own... or you'll never know if it's you he loves...*

If only Granddad could meet Jake and tell her what she wanted to hear. *This one is different.* Jake didn't need or want her money. He loved her, rich or poor. In truth, she thought he'd like it better if she were poor. If he didn't want marriage, so be it. They'd be together; that's what mat-

tered. Besides, she'd exchanged vows before and look what
happened.

Catherine closed her eyes. "Please God, don't let me be
wrong again."

The old radiator under the window hissed to life. It was
only late September, but the draft off the windows warned
winter was just around the corner.

Jake packed his meager belongings into the last of the
cardboard boxes, then stood tall, arching and rubbing the
small of his sore back. A black and battered suitcase plus
two boxes sat apart from the others. Those he'd take to
Aunt Helen's where he'd share a room with Sarge until the
closing on the house. The rest he'd store downstairs. The
Salvation Army was coming by later for the dinette set and
lumpy brown sofa. *Damn.* He wished the sofa didn't have
to go. Feeling overly sentimental, he went to the sink and
cupped water in his hands, drinking some, then splashing
the rest on his face.

Cat's drawings lay on the counter next to him and he gave
them a cursory glance, having already committed every line
and angle to memory. Why hadn't he thought of this before? The answer to his money problems had been right under his nose all along.

He hoisted a box onto his shoulder and picked up the
suitcase, a smile lingering on his lips as he made his way
down the stairs. Most of the money he'd saved for Sally was
now committed to renovating Top Cat—a name Cat had so
cleverly suggested. If he pressed hard, it wouldn't take long
before those old hardwood floors would be pulsating to the
beat of line dancers from all over the city.

Jake ran up and down the stairs a few more times, then
stood in the doorway catching his breath. He'd see this place
many times in the future, but it would never be the same.
That was okay, he decided, nodding his head. It never really felt like home, anyway. It was simply a convenient place
to crash at the end of the day. His gaze lingered on the
lumpy sofa. He'd miss that old thing, though, and the
memories it evoked. Exhausted, Jake decided to give it a
proper farewell.

He strolled over to it and spread horizontally, squirming into just the right dips and mounds. He closed his eyes and pictured Cat beside him. It was here she'd assured him it didn't matter what he had, or didn't have, he was the man she loved.

Strange. During all their loving and planning, she never brought up marriage. Was she old-fashioned enough that she was waiting for him to broach the subject first? Probably. Usually such talk came before house buying. He chuckled aloud as he struggled to his feet. Why should he be surprised? They hadn't done anything in the usual order. Hell, they'd already been on their honeymoon.

He carried the last load to the Jeep and thought about a place in Waterford packing them in with free dance lessons. Top Cat was far enough away to draw its own crowd. In no time at all this decision could pay off. Not in time for his money-grubbing ex, but that was okay. He had that part worked out, too.

Jake jumped behind the wheel of the Jeep and stared at the second floor. If he legally separated the two floors into two independent businesses he could sell off Top Cat. Cash from the sale of the upper floor combined with the balance of his savings could net enough to satisfy Sally's debt. Finding a buyer could be tricky, but he had two ideas already.

He let out a low chuckle. Sarge and Charlie—won't they be surprised. But they spend enough time at Alley Cat that one of them may as well have a piece of the action. With the new elevator being installed, the last obstacle would be eliminated for Sarge. And Jake was pretty sure either of the men had the money it would take. One of them just might jump on the chance.

He started the engine and frowned. Of course that would mean telling one or both of them that he needed to act fast since he was pressed for cash and the deadline was approaching—facts he'd kept from both of them.

All he had to do was swallow his damnable pride.

He drove off, feeling depressed. Maybe he'd think of another way.

Eleven

―――――

"I hope you like sawdust." Jake hunched the phone to one shoulder and wiped his eyes with a handkerchief. "It's everywhere."

"In your eyebrows?" She giggled, sounding as happy as he felt, although his back ached from using muscles he'd forgotten he had.

"Among other places." Her laugh was light and familiar and he wondered how he could wait until tonight to see her. "So how are things going at Top Cat? You learn how to use a hammer and paintbrush yet?"

"I think I'm holding my own, but you'll have to ask the crew that question."

He heard hammering in the background and chuckled. "I already have. They say your specs and drawings are better than most architects."

"Darn tootin'!"

Now Jake laughed in earnest. "Darn tootin'?"

"Aunt Helen stopped by and gave her approval. One

carpenter said I worked as hard as any man. That's when she said..."

"Darn tootin'. I should've known." He listened to Cat answer one of the men's questions and beamed with pride. Top Cat would be done long before their house. She had proved to herself what he knew all along. She'll love working with *Habitat for Humanity,* and they'll love having her.

"Talk to you later, handsome. I have to get back to work," she said.

Before she could hang up he said, "Did you bring a change of clothes?"

"Yes, sir. And they haven't ripped your shower out yet. Are we still on for this mystery night out?"

"Darn tootin'. I'll pick you up around six."

"I'll be ready."

Catherine dressed quickly behind the only partition still standing. Sore muscles were ignored as adrenaline pumped through her veins. Could this mystery night be what she suspected?

By the time she jumped into the Jeep next to Jake, she thought her skin might actually burst. Only eleven hours since she'd seen him but it seemed longer. He leaned across the console and she threw her arms around his neck. She pressed her cheek next to his. He smelled of shampoo and after-shave. She brushed her lips on his neck as his large hands trailed gently down her arms.

This was home. Not the house she was raised in, not even the one they would soon share. It was Jake. Jake was home. Wherever that may take her.

When she loosened her grip on his neck and sat back, Jake appraised her from head to toe and back again to her face. Beyond the moisture in his eyes she saw the look that he sometimes tried to hide—the deep, penetrating view of his pure and loving soul.

They sat there for what seemed to be the longest time, until Jake finally smiled his slanted smile.

"When I retire I might go up north fishing for a day or two."

A laugh burst deep from Catherine, releasing the almost-unbearable emotions she'd contained behind her rib cage. "What on earth are you talking about?"

"I suppose you'll want to go to New York now and then to see some play I don't give two hoots about." His smile faded and he gazed deep into her eyes. "But besides that, never will we be far apart."

Catherine met his steady gaze, then moved closer, brushing his lips softly with her own. "You got that right, cowboy." She forced herself not to cry and gave him a mischievous wink. "Except for one thing."

He looked down his nose at her in mock warning. "Oh yeah, and what would that be?"

She lifted her chin, not backing away. "I might want to go fishing *with* you." Jake laughed, the deep, husky laugh she never tired of hearing. She sat back and he grabbed the gearshift.

"*That* I'd have to see."

Ten minutes later, they turned off Woodward and headed east on 696, heat blasting from the dash along with one of their favorite Reba McEntire tapes. When they exited onto 75 and continued toward downtown Detroit, Catherine wondered where they were going. Until now, she hadn't paid the slightest attention or cared.

Jake turned down the volume. "Figure it out yet?"

"Haven't a clue."

Jake reached over and patted her knee. By the wry smile he flashed her before returning his attention to the freeway, she thought her suspicions had been confirmed. She settled back in her seat and swallowed a smug smile. As hard as she'd tried convincing herself marriage wasn't that important, she hadn't succeeded. More than anything, she wanted that final commitment. She could barely wait to hear the words.

But wait they did—while checking into the Westin Hotel, thrashing around the bed in an urgent explosion of love and passion, and even through cocktails and dinner. Side by side, they dined leisurely at the Summit, the top floor of the

Westin, the highest point of the center tower snuggled amidst the glass cluster known as the Renaissance Center. They talked about their current projects and more about Catherine's ideas for *Habitat*.

Finally, the table cleared and coffee served, Jake eyed her and worried. He'd made such a big production of this night would she be disappointed there wasn't more? Was she expecting words he couldn't say yet? Maybe he should have waited.

He stretched both arms across the back of their crescent-shaped booth and gazed out onto the Detroit River and the lights of Windsor beyond. Behind them and seventy floors below, was Belle Isle. As the revolving floor of the Summit made its slow rotation, he fretted and watched the flashing light atop the Fischer Building, and the General Motors building, Greektown and a host of other familiar landmarks, finally deciding the gift in his pocket should wait until he could ask the question that went with it.

But Catherine had other ideas.

"Well?" she blurted out. "Are you going to give it to me or what?"

Excitement danced in her eyes and Jake knew he was in trouble.

"I've been watching that bulge in your jacket pocket all night and wondering if it was for me."

"Oh?" He smiled at Cat, knowing there was no turning back now. "Is that what you were looking at?"

"Oh, you." She waved her hand at him, her gaze still fixed on his pocket.

Hesitantly he retrieved the small black velvet box, groping for words that might salvage the situation. "I . . . I was going to wait till your birthday next weekend . . . but since we'll be at your parents, well . . ."

Jake looked down at the box in his hands and back to her loving face, hoping she wouldn't be too disappointed.

"Sarge gave me this just before . . ." He was about to say "Just before he married Sally," but the words didn't seem right. He started again. "My father gave this to me a long time ago. It belonged to his mother, my grandmother. She died when I was a baby so I never got to know her. Sarge always said she was a very special lady...and that someday, if I ever found my own special lady, I might want her to have it."

He hesitated one last time. Then, his eyes not leaving hers, he slipped the velvet box into her hands and closed them around it. Her skin was soft and warm. Her fingers began to tremble and he tightened his grip to still them. With his eyes he tried to tell her what was in his heart. He lifted his hands from hers and nodded for her to open the box.

Cautiously she lifted it, handling it as though it were fragile and priceless. Slowly she raised the lid. Her eyes sparkled with moisture, shining brighter than the tiny diamonds that outlined the heart-shaped emerald she held. Catherine stared at it in total rapture.

"Jake..." Her voice was deep and hoarse. "Oh, Jake." She met his gaze as a tear trickled down her cheek. "It's the most beautiful gift I've ever received." Clutching the box to her chest with one hand, she pulled his face to hers with the other. She kissed him as she never had before. Gently, tenderly, lingering there with eyes opened, inches from his, sending her message straight to his soul. He'd never loved her more than he did this very moment.

He pulled her close to him and held her there until the blurriness in his own eyes cleared. Her arms were wrapped so tightly around his back that his sore muscles began to ache and he eased her from him.

Taking the box from her, he removed the ring and slipped it onto the third finger of her left hand. She straightened her arm and studied it, her approval obvious.

Jake leaned back against the booth and sighed. From time to time Cat eyed him curiously, as if she expected more. Eventually her gaze settled on her left hand.

A stab of guilt poked at Jake's ribs. He'd convinced himself he was too busy working on the house to talk with Sarge and Charlie. If he hadn't put it off, maybe he could have asked Cat the question he was longing to ask.

Jake looked back at her, fingering her gift and smiling wistfully. If only he had told her about his money problem, she'd understand his hesitation in proposing tonight. It wasn't really a secret. It just never seemed the right time.

Catherine nuzzled closer to his side and wrapped her arm around his waist. If she was disappointed she hid it well. Jake kissed the top of her head and made a decision. Pride be damned. He'd talk to his father tomorrow. With a little luck he'd be able to ask Cat to marry him soon and all would be right with the world.

So what was the point in bringing up old debts now?

When he asked Sarge the next day, his father was more than interested. He was downright excited with the idea. Getting back to work would add years to his life, he'd said. And with the good investments he'd made over the years since selling Alley Cat, he had more than enough ready cash to close the deal.

And so it was agreed. As quickly as the papers could be drawn up, Top Cat would be Sarge's.

The next night, in the bare living room of what would be their new home, Jake finally asked the big question. When Catherine just stared at him and didn't answer, his heart beat faster. Had he been wrong in assuming she wanted marriage, too? "So? Will you?" he asked again, trying to keep his voice even.

"Yes," she finally said, then turned her attention to her new ring. "Though I should've taken a couple days to give you an answer...since you made me wait so long to hear the question." She was twisting her hand, catching moon-beams with the diamonds, her brilliant smile competing with its reflection.

Jake studied the beautiful creature sitting cross-legged in the middle of the floor beside him. He'd thought maybe to-night he'd tell her about Sally and how he'd arranged to pay off the debt, but seeing her serene happiness, he decided against it. There were more enjoyable things to discuss now that she'd agreed to marry him.

Purposefully he remained silent and let Cat be the first to speak.

Eventually she lowered her left hand and turned to him. "So, when can we talk about the wedding?"

His smile was one of victory, knowing he'd outwaited her. "I figured you had it all worked out. I was just waiting to hear the details."

She punched him playfully in the chest. "You're insufferable, you know that?"

"Is that what all that noise was about earlier? I'm just a big pain in the..."

"You're just a big tease, Jake Alley, and don't pretend you don't know it. Why else would you give me a ring then wait forty-eight hours to propose?"

Jake leaned his elbows on his raised knees and dodged the bullet. "So tell me—what's the plan?"

When she'd finished a few minutes later, his smile disappeared, replaced by a slack jaw and openmouthed stare. "You're serious about this? You're not putting me on now, are you?"

Catherine folded her arms across her chest. "Unless you got a better idea, I think it would be fun."

Jake leaned back, slapped his knees and shook his head. "You're just full of surprises, aren't you?" He laughed his low laugh, obviously warming to Catherine's plan. "If Aunt Helen were here, she'd say you were full of piss and vinegar."

"Aunt Helen already knows that. She was at the reception when I made my little announcement. Remember?"

"Who could forget?" He took Catherine's left hand and fingered his grandmother's ring. When he looked up he eyed Cat evenly. "It won't be like the last time, Cat. I would never hurt you."

She swallowed hard before she spoke. "I know that, Jake." She studied his hand on hers. "One of the many things I love about you is your honesty. I know you would never abuse my trust." Then smiling up at him she lightened her tone. "Why, you don't have a deceitful bone in your body."

Jake kept his gaze on her hand, then lifted her fingers to his lips, avoiding her eyes. Someday he'd tell her why he waited to propose, but now wasn't the time.

"So, you ready to don the suit and meet my family next Saturday?"

Jake sat back, relieved the subject had been changed. "I don't seem to have much choice, do I?" He looked around, feigning nervousness, which wasn't much of an act.

"Relax, sweetheart, after Saturday night we're home free. We'll have my inheritance and our announcement behind us. Nothing but happy ever after to follow."

Her inheritance. Another thing to worry about. "Tell me. What does a guy buy his lady for her birthday when she's about to have more money than she knows what to do with?" He tried sounding breezy and confident, but she saw right through him.

Cat wrapped her arms around his neck and pulled him closer. "Don't worry about it, cowboy. There's something you can give me that no one else ever can."

There was a catch in his throat when he held her away from him and spoke. "Do I have to wait till your birthday to give it to you?" A moment later her laugh disappeared on his lips.

At dusk the following Saturday, Catherine's birthday, Jake pulled his Jeep into the circular driveway and sat staring at the sprawling Tudor mansion at the end of the long slate walk. What had he gotten himself into now?

He tugged at his tie, remembering the last time he wore one was the night this all began. Would her parents recognize him from the wedding? Did they know he went with her to Jamaica? He wished he'd thought to ask Catherine these questions earlier. It was this house, he told himself. And the money—however much she was about to inherit, she hadn't said and he didn't ask. This whole scene was unnerving. He wasn't certain about anything at the moment, except that he loved Catherine as no other woman he'd ever known. For now, that would have to do.

Exhaling a nervous sigh, he picked up the red roses on the passenger seat and strode toward the front door. An elderly black woman in a black uniform with a crisp white apron opened the massive oak door and ushered him in.

"Miss Catherine will be right down, Mr. Jake." The old woman gave him a conspiratorial wink and a big, toothy smile. He wondered how much Catherine had told her.

"You must be Ellie." He shifted the flowers to his left hand and stuck out his right. "Nice to meet you."

Ellie looked at his hand a moment, seeming uncertain. Then she smiled again and shook it.

"Nice to meet you, too, Mr. Jake."

Terrific! The servants already know he's a country bumpkin. How long before... He spotted Catherine gliding soundlessly down the long winding staircase flashing her perfect smile at him and for the moment he forgot about his lack of social graces. She wore a black, lacy dress, the jagged points of the hem flitting around her knees. Her shoulders were bare and a single strand of pearls graced her long neck. She held his gaze as she descended, not speaking. When she reached the bottom step, she held out her hand and he took it, speechless.

What was he doing here, with this gorgeous creature looking at him the way she was? Ellie made a graceful exit and he finally braved a few words.

"These are for you." He held out the bouquet and she took it, burying her face in its center, inhaling deeply.

"They're beautiful, Jake," she said, returning her gaze to his.

"Not nearly as beautiful as you." It was true. But as soon as the words were out, he felt the heat on his neck and knew it was traveling to his face. *Damn!* He felt like such a klutz. If he was going to survive this night, he'd better find the real Jake Alley. Fast.

He straightened his back and tried again.

"Happy birthday, Catherine." He rested his hands on her bare shoulders and kissed her gently on the cheek. Had the roses not been between them, he may have crushed her to him and kissed her again. Not so gently. When he backed away, he stared at her face.

"Stop it," he said.

"Stop what?" She lifted her chin and widened her smile.

"You know very well what. Seducing me." He tried to sound stern, but he knew the corners of his lips were twitching.

She held one hand to her chest. *"Moi?"*

"You can hide whatever you're feeling, gorgeous," he said eyeing the length of her dress. "But it's not so easy for me."

Her gaze darted to below his belt and up again. She laughed and was about to speak just as her parents entered the foyer.

Quickly Catherine stepped to Jake's side, held the bouquet in front of his pants, and made her introductions. Jake shook hands, feeling like a Roman hiding behind a fig leaf. Fortunately, without lingering conversation, Mason led the way to the study, his wife beside him.

Catherine looked like a schoolgirl swallowing a giggle in church. Jake took her elbow and gave her a warning squeeze as they followed close behind.

The room was large but cozy. A fire burned behind the stone hearth. Jake looked at the logs, expecting gas, surprised to find real wood. Tall walls were topped with ornate molding below a coved ceiling and mostly hidden by highly polished mahogany bookshelves full of hard-covered books.

To the far left was a round, lace-covered table in front of a large bay window overlooking a garden. Jake noticed the four place settings, ready and waiting, and he let out a slow breath. The thought of sitting at a long, formal dining table had been cause for a fitful drive over. He wondered whose idea the less formal setting was as Catherine tugged him over Oriental rugs to the opposite end of the room.

A love seat faced the fireplace, flanked by a pair of leather wing chairs—one a deep wine, the other dark green. Catherine's father took what was obviously his seat—the green one on the left with an antique pipe stand next to it, while Mrs. Mason sat in the other. Jake and Catherine settled side by side on the sofa. They all eyed each other a moment and then Mason rose again, rubbing his hands together and smiling.

"What can I get everyone to drink?" He looked to his wife first.

"A glass of white wine would be lovely," she said softly.

"Catherine?"

"I'll have the same."

Finally he turned to Jake, a smile firmly in place. "And you, Jake. What would you care for?"

Jake felt three pairs of eyes riveted on him. Shaking Ellie's hand was probably mistake number one. This was surely number two. But what the hey.

"I'll have a beer." He glanced at Catherine and she smiled her approval.

"Beer it is," Mason said, and went to the bar section of one wall unit. Jake watched as he poured two glasses of wine. Then he pulled a bottle of Heineken from a bucket of ice, uncapped it and filled a tall glass.

Surprised, Jake looked back at Catherine, whose face told him she'd never make a good poker player. If beer had been the wrong answer, you'd never know it. Jake took the proffered glass and a moment later hoisted it in the air with the others.

"To our lovely daughter whom we both cherish dearly," her father began and Jake saw the shine in the older man's eyes. "Happy thirtieth birthday, Catherine. May this day bring you the happiness you so richly deserve."

Jake lifted his glass and took a small swallow, wishing he could down the whole thing. It was hard to hear the word *richly* without wondering *how rich?* Not too long ago he thought Catherine might be another woman after his money. Now her parents were probably having similar thoughts about him. And how could he blame them? Thinking about their surprise announcement later, he swallowed a smirk with another slug of beer.

Mason set his brandy down and faced Jake squarely. His arms rested on his knees and for the longest time he said nothing. Jake returned his gaze evenly, letting Cat's father take his measure. He had nothing to hide. He loved this man's daughter and he tried to convey it without words. Out of the corner of his eye, Jake saw Catherine's head turn to her father, then to Jake, then back again to her father. After what seemed an eternity Mason spoke, not to his daughter, but to Jake.

"My wife and I have discussed this with Catherine." He glanced at his wife and Jake followed his gaze. She was smiling warmly at her daughter, looking wistful.

"It was our daughter's decision to share this important event with you," Mason continued. "In a moment, I'm sure you will realize the significance of her trust." He looked back to his wife.

Ceremoniously, she stood and walked toward Catherine. In her hands was a small brown booklet about the size and thickness of a passport. Catherine took it from her mother's outstretched hand as she bent to kiss her daughter on the forehead. There were tears in both women's eyes as mother returned to her chair and daughter fingered the gold engraved letters on the cover.

Jake looked at the lettering and read the raised words.

National Bank of Detroit.

Mason looked first to his daughter, then to Jake, where he hesitated for only a moment. "Catherine informed us that you are aware of her inheritance."

Jake nodded, seeing the understandable wariness in the man's eyes, and Mason pressed on.

"My father, Catherine's grandfather, was a very successful man." He shifted his weight and crossed his legs, warming to his subject. "He was also very wise. He saw how wealth had destroyed the children and grandchildren of some of his friends and he was determined not to let that happen to his family.

"When I was young, he paid for my education and necessary living expenses but he insisted I work part-time for the extras. At the time, I may have thought he was unnecessarily hard on me, since he had more money than he could ever spend. But eventually I came to understand and appreciate his wisdom."

Jake looked at Catherine and saw the moisture in her eyes. And for a moment, the unabashed love between the two made him feel as if he were an intruder. But then Mason shared his gaze with Jake, making him feel a welcome part. Catherine took his hand in hers, squeezing it hard and meaningfully.

"Unlike you, Catherine, I had no idea that my thirtieth birthday would bring such a gift. But I'm proud to say that your knowledge of this inevitable day has not tarnished you in the least. You have worked hard and learned the value of a dollar earned." He leaned back and picked up his brandy, swishing its contents. Then he looked at his wife and the two shared the last moments of what was obviously their little secret.

Jake looked directly into Catherine's eyes for the first time since they sat down. She only smiled and shrugged. Then her mother broke the silence.

"Your father's having fun with this, dear, but it's time you learn the amount, don't you think?"

Jake looked from one to the other, then settled on Catherine who held the booklet tentatively in her right hand. Before she opened it, she gazed up at Jake, searching his face for the answer to a question she hadn't asked.

It took a beat, but then he understood.

He smiled down at her, tightening his hold on her hand, and did his best to allay her doubts. It didn't matter how much money she had. Nothing would change between them.

Slowly she removed her hand from his. Jake watched her fingers tremble as she turned the pages to the last entry.

The tension in the room was nearly palpable as awareness seeped into the pair on the sofa. Yes, they had both known there was a large inheritance. But neither had guessed *how* large.

Jake had expected to see six zeros, at least five. Slowly, for the second time, he counted right to left. He'd been right the first time.

Seven zeros. Seven zeros?

Incredulously Jake looked up from the page to Catherine's face. Her eyes were large. Her mouth open. She stared at the page in stunned silence as if she couldn't believe the number, either.

Finally she lifted her head. First she looked at her father, long and hard, his face appearing more than a little pleased that she'd been surprised. By the time she looked at her mother, tears were streaming down both women's faces.

Then Catherine turned and took Jake's hand in both of hers. She studied his face once again, almost pleading for reassurance. If they'd been alone, he would have held her close and said the words she needed to hear. But her parents were there. Waiting. Watching. He was expected to say something, of that much he was certain. But what?

Unable to stand the drama another second, Jake stared at the ceiling and let out a loud breath. Then he looked back at Catherine's frightened face.

"From now on, Ms. Mason, whenever you stop by Alley Cat, you're buying your own drinks."

Catherine flung her arms around his neck and began to sob. He patted her on the back and let her rock him side to side. He glanced briefly at her parents. They were smiling at each other, sharing their own private moment.

When the flood subsided, Catherine removed the handkerchief from Jake's breast pocket, dabbed at her cheeks, then gave a good blow. Quick glances flitted around the room and then suddenly they all began to laugh.

Mason got up first and pulled his daughter into a warm embrace, her mother pushing him gently aside for her turn. When Catherine stepped back, she was smiling broadly. She looked from one loved one to the next, finally stopping on her mother's face.

"When do we eat? I'm starved."

Her mother stared at her watch with a look of panic. "Oh, my goodness. We barely have an hour before your other guests arrive." She flashed a quick smile, then retreated toward the kitchen, calling over her shoulder, "Everyone take a seat . . . I'll tell Ellie we're ready."

Twelve

Catherine pushed broccoli pieces around her plate with her fork, half listening to Jake and her father. Conversation flowed easily between them, mostly about Catherine's plans for *Habitat*.

"Are you enjoying the construction work at Top Cat?" her father asked.

It took a couple of beats before his words registered. "Y-yes, I am," she managed weakly. Catherine felt her mother studying her face.

"You've barely touched your dinner, dear. Is something wrong?"

Catherine pushed out her chair and stood, ignoring the question and posing one of her own. "Since we're finished, why don't we help Ellie and clear the table?" She looked at her mother. "I know you'll feel much better if these dirty dishes are out of sight before anyone arrives."

"Jake is a guest, dear." She waved her hand for him to find a more comfortable seat near the fire.

"I don't mind. Let me help," he said.

Catherine pretended not to notice the curious look Jake shot her as they made their way to the kitchen. Maybe tonight's announcement wasn't such a good one, after all, she thought. They'd already had enough excitement for one night. Her stomach was in knots. If only she'd told them about Jake earlier—how much he'd come to mean to her in such a short time. How could she expect them to understand . . .

When they entered the kitchen Ellie spun around, the whites of her eyes bulging with distress. She purposefully spread her arms out in an obvious attempt to conceal something behind her.

"Jus—jus' set the dishes down anywhere. I'll take care of 'em later." Her eyes implored Catherine for help, but it was too late. The lady of the house had a curiosity that couldn't be denied.

"What are you hiding back there, Ellie?" Catherine's mother asked.

"It's okay, Ellie," Catherine sighed. "Let everyone see."

Embarrassed, Ellie stepped aside as they all gathered round. Ellie had made Catherine a chocolate sheet cake with chocolate frosting and pink lettering—a birthday tradition that was as old as Catherine herself. Only this year the words were different. The top line read, On This Special Day. In itself not too revealing—except the first letter was in the shape of a large diamond ring, and in the center were two intertwined hearts. The bottom line read, Love And Happiness Always. Out of the corner of her eye, Catherine watched her parents as awareness stole their smiles, leaving them pale and rigid at her side.

Before she could find her voice, her mother pulled Catherine into a tight embrace, her voice husky with emotion when she spoke over her daughter's shoulder. "Engaged on your birthday! Won't your guests be surprised."

Tentatively, her father stepped forward and shook Jake's hand. "Congratulations."

"Thank you," Jake said, glancing over at Catherine, sending her a look that said, "Remember, this was your idea."

"Dad," Catherine began, her voice quavering. "I know all this is sudden, but you'll have to trust I know what I'm doing—" she swallowed hard and added "—this time." His brow remained furrowed, but she pushed on. "Would you and Mom make the official announcement after our guests arrive?"

Her father studied her from the side of his face, one eyebrow arched, then asked, "You sure about this, Catherine?"

Squaring her shoulders, she forced her voice above a whisper. "Yes. I am."

Their gazes locked on each other before he spoke again.

"Then so be it." He hugged her quickly and started back to the study, his hand on Jake's shoulder.

"After the announcement Ellie can bring out the cake," Catherine called after them. Knees shaking, she turned around. Ellie was leaning against the sink with her head down. Catherine walked over and gave Ellie's arm a reassuring squeeze. "The cake's beautiful, Ellie. Everything is just fine." She winked and put on her best smile before leaving the kitchen, all the time wishing someone could reassure her that she was doing the right thing.

Catherine could hear the two men talking as they ambled down the hall in search of new logs for the fire. She helped her mother fold in the corners of the soiled linen tablecloth, careful not to spill crumbs onto the round Persian rug.

Finally her mother balled the cloth against her chest and looked at Catherine. "He's a very nice young man, Catherine . . ."

"But?" She heard it in her mother's voice.

"I only hope you have a long engagement period—at least a year or so—get to know each other well before—"

"Before I make another mistake?" she finished, not meaning to sound as curt as she had. Why was she so tense? Everything was working out fine. "I'm sorry, Mom," she said, wishing she could have a good cry and get it out of her system.

"So am I, Catherine. You're a grown woman. Surely you know what you're doing." She walked around the table. "Come on, show me your ring. You've been sitting on it all night and I'm tired of trying to sneak peeks."

The doorbell rang and Ellie brushed passed them. "Company's here," she called out as she waddled to the front door.

Aunt Helen had just finished introducing Jake's father and Charlie when Becky arrived. Catherine greeted her best friend warmly and repeated introductions. She suddenly realized how long it had been since she and Becky had had a real heart-to-heart. She wished there was time for one right now to calm her nerves. But there wasn't. What would Becky think when she heard the news of another engagement so soon? Catherine wondered again if things were moving too fast. She looked hard at Jake as he walked down the hall sharing a joke with Sarge and Charlie. Who was this man? And how had he captured her heart and soul so quickly and completely?

Sometime during her reverie everyone had wandered into the study, leaving her alone with her mother who looked around anxiously.

"I realize Uncle Will isn't here yet, but Ellie said he couldn't make it until later. Since he's the only guest missing, would you like Dad and I to make the announcement now? Or would you rather we wait?"

Catherine snapped out of her funk and hugged her mother, then ushered her inside. "Tell Daddy we're ready."

Minutes later when Jake rejoined her, Catherine stared at the floor, still fighting the urge to cry. Why couldn't she just relax and enjoy this special night? Maybe she was being overly sensitive, but something didn't feel right. Earlier she'd floated through dinner, as nervous as any woman might be, but knowing she'd made the right decision. Now, standing here hand in hand with Jake, she thought back over the past few days. He'd seemed so distracted and sometimes short with her over nothing. Today they hadn't seen each other until he showed up at the door. Each had their last-minute errands. She was arranging her surprise gift for him, and he ... what *was* he doing? She'd gone to the house twice, certain she'd find him there when he wasn't at Alley Cat, but the workers said they hadn't seen him all day.

Suddenly Catherine heard her father's final words... *the future Mr. and Mrs. Jake Alley!* A hush fell over the room as all faces turned in her direction. Everything appeared in slow motion—familiar faces, stunned, openmouthed. Just like that other awful night...

Then there was thunderous applause and those same faces were smiling and rushing to her. Closer and closer. She felt her knees buckle.

Jake gripped her around the waist and held her tight. "Are you okay, sweetheart?"

She looked up at him, stunned for a moment at the face she saw. It wasn't TJ. It was Jake. She sucked in air and felt the panic subside.

"I...I'm fine. Just excited, I guess." She accepted the first of many hugs and well wishes, telling herself she *would* be fine. It was just the memory of that horrible reception that was playing havoc with her emotions tonight. That, and the fact that they'd had little sleep over the past weeks, working day and night. She was being a silly goose, she told herself.

"Can I get you something to drink?" Jake asked.

"Maybe some Coke," she said, feeling better.

"Coke?"

"I've had enough champagne. Think I'll coast awhile."

"Coke it is, then." He squeezed her hand and departed for the bar.

Mrs. Alley. Mrs. Jake Alley. Cat Alley. Alley Cat.

She remembered playing this game before in Jamaica. Who would have thunk? She smiled, feeling a little guilty over her doubts. Jake and TJ were as different as day and night. She trusted Jake. She chuckled aloud at a strange thought. If she surveyed the room as to whom each trusted more—a bartender or a lawyer—she knew who'd win.

Jake returned with her Coke and handed it to her, planting a loud kiss on her lips as he did. "What's so funny?"

She hooked her arm in his and smiled. "I'll tell you later." She'd been foolish to worry. Everything was perfect. Even her inheritance didn't seem to be a problem. "So...what were you up to all day?" she asked, changing the subject.

"Oh, a little of this, little of that. Taking care of business." Charlie came and the pair walked off, sharing a joke.

What business? she wanted to ask, but he was gone. A tightness started in the pit of her stomach and spread to her chest. Maybe he was arranging a surprise gift—like she had for him. Or maybe it was something else. Something he didn't want her to know. Suddenly she felt nauseous, her legs spongy and weak. Images of another night and TJ flitted across her memory. She shook herself and swore under her breath. If she didn't get control of her wavering emotions, this night would be a disaster. And it would be all her fault. TJ was the past. Jake was now. And always.

She spotted Ellie bringing out the cake and told herself to get a grip. The singing that ensued brought a small smile to Catherine's lips. When Charlie started a second refrain of "Happy engagement to you..." Catherine felt her worries slip away as drinks were refreshed and the party resumed. Jake would tell her later what he was up to today and she'd feel foolish for worrying. She was making a mountain out of a molehill.

Aunt Helen stopped at her side. She sniffled and pulled out her ever-present lace hankie. "This is so romantic. I can't wait for the wedding." She honked into her handkerchief and Jake laughed as he joined the pair.

"Aunt Helen...you and your weddings." Jake smiled at her fondly, then hoisted his glass in her direction.

Catherine's mother was next to jump in, aiming her question at Jake. "Speaking of weddings, do you mind if we talk about it?"

Jake winked at her before looking down to Cat. "Do I have any choice?"

Cat elbowed him in the side and turned to her mother. "Don't let him kid you, Mom. He's dying to hear your ideas."

And so the evening continued. The women talked excitedly about flowers and clothes and food while the men eyed each other and pretended to be bored.

Catherine's mother had Aunt Helen's rapt attention. "When the time comes, she could walk down our winding staircase then down the hall to here. Jake could be waiting there—" she pointed to the stone hearth "—amidst a candlelit forest of white roses. The vows should be short and traditional." Aunt Helen's head bobbed agreement. "Maybe Uncle Will could perform the ceremony. My brother's a judge, you know." Aunt Helen's eyebrows arched.

Catherine's mother looked at her watch and frowned. "Where is he, anyway? What could be keeping him?"

Charlie piped in. "Maybe he had to sign a warrant or something. On TV they're always goin' to some judge's house to get him to sign something."

Everyone laughed, including Charlie who rubbed his hands together, appearing pleased that he had everyone's attention. "I have another wedding idea if anyone wants to hear it." The group gathered closer, encouraging him.

"If they got married on New Year's Eve the reception could be at Top Cat. Grand opening, New Year's celebration and wedding reception. All rolled into one."

Catherine's mother fingered the pearls at her neck. "Of course you mean a *year* from this New Year's Eve."

Charlie hesitated only a moment. "Of course. Right."

"Ooh. I like that idea," she said, relieved. "The invitations could read Western Garb Mandatory. Black Tie Not Optional." The laughter escalated and Catherine's father picked up from there.

"We could throw a New Year's Eve theme party, albeit an unusual one for our social circle, but I hear this line dancing business is becoming the 'in' thing."

Catherine strolled over to the bay window and Jake followed. When he slipped his arm around her shoulder she spoke straight ahead. "They have some pretty good ideas. Do you think we should reconsider our plan?"

There was a long pause then he said, "If I didn't know better, I'd think you were getting cold feet."

She looked up into his dark eyes, suddenly serious and more than a little anxious. How could she have any doubts about this kind and gentle man? If he was withholding anything, it was probably some surprise, not unlike what she had planned for him later. She reached up and touched his cheek.

"I'm just being an overly emotional female, that's all." She flung her arms around his neck and held him close. Searching for words that would lighten the mood, she came up with only one thought. "Is the Jeep out front? Gassed and ready to go?" she whispered.

He kissed the top of her head and whispered back, "To borrow a phrase—darn tootin'. Besides, it's the only way you know how to leave a party."

She backed away smiling and poked him in the chest, just as her mother called out. "Come on, Jake. We're going on a tour of the house. Join us." Catherine watched him roll his eyes and walk away with the others. Charlie begged off, staying with Sarge by the fire.

Catherine turned back to the window and smiled up at the clear black night, thanking the Powers above. A man she loved who loved her, who was honest and true. A man who kept no secrets from her—oh, maybe a little surprise or two—but a person who would never deceive her.

Charlie walked up beside her. Overcome with happiness she threw her arms around him and kissed his cheek. Then she whispered, "Is everything all set for later?" She looked up into his smiling eyes.

"Don't you worry about a thing." He smiled conspiratorially and she mouthed the words, "Thank you," as he headed back to Sarge.

While everyone was occupied, Catherine decided to find Ellie and thank her for the delicious cake and to assure her its early unveiling hadn't been a problem.

When Catherine walked down the hall to the study a few minutes later, she could hear Charlie's and Sarge's muted voices. Their backs were to her and they didn't notice her in the doorway. One more step and she came to an abrupt halt.

It was just two words—*Jake* and *money*—but everything inside her stiffened.

She stood very still, not wanting them to see her and hating herself for eavesdropping. But with a sudden sense of foreboding, she had to know what this was all about.

Sarge said, "I wish he'd told me sooner that things were so bad. Another couple weeks and he would've lost Alley Cat."

Catherine stepped back into the hallway not wanting to believe her ears. Her mind raced for a logical explanation.

Then she heard Charlie speak. "Leave it to clever ol' Jake to find a way out." Catherine felt the walls closing in. "Now he'll be debt free and have all the money he needs." Charlie slapped Sarge on the back. "All's well that ends well!" Glasses clinked as the pair laughed.

Catherine had heard enough. Her inner voice had been right all night. It wasn't just nerves. Oh, God. How could this be happening again? Maybe this time she could just slip out the door unnoticed.

But her legs wouldn't move. She withdrew deeper into herself, searching for that safe, neutral zone, where she was simply an observer, a place where her mind could float free, letting inane thoughts tumble and churn, blocking out anything real or logical. After a moment, she felt the numbing sensation take over, erasing any sense that her body occupied space.

As the others filed back into the study, Catherine watched in stony silence. She'd been here before. The same faces walking merrily around, oblivious to the impending disaster. It reminded her of that movie, *Groundhog Day*. How many more times would she relive this scene? Until she got it right?

She saw Jake crossing to her and the fog cleared. He was smiling, coming closer.

Reality returned with a vengeance. Anger pumped through her veins like a tornado gaining speed.

She pushed Jake aside with a hard left elbow and marched toward the fireplace. She heard him behind her, calling her name, closing the distance between them. It didn't matter. *He* didn't matter. He wasn't the Jake she thought he was.

She spun around to face the others when Jake stepped in front of her, blocking their view.

"Cat . . . what's wrong?"

How could he look so innocent? "You know perfectly well what's wrong."

"I've seen this look before and I don't like it."

He was beginning to sound angry. It was the old "best defense is a good offense" routine. Well, it wasn't going to work on her. She leaned into him. "You lied to me, Jake Alley."

Jake raised his voice. "What the hell are you talking about?"

The room fell silent. She wished she could spare everyone this scene. But it had started. She had to finish. Nonetheless, she kept her voice as low as she could.

"I overheard a little conversation tonight, Mr. I-Don't-Need-Your-Money." Finally she saw a crack in his armor, a flicker of recognition. That's all she needed to confirm her worst fears. "A rich wife would solve all your problems." Tears streaked down her face, which only made her angrier. She didn't want him to see her pain. She looked away only to see the faces of those she loved. The same faces as before. Eyes wide, mouths slack. She turned back to Jake, wishing she'd just walked out when she'd had the chance.

Jake gripped her shoulders. She tried to shrug him off, but he tightened his hold. "Listen to me. I wanted to tell you. There just hasn't been a right time."

His eyes were sad and she hated him for it. "Oh, yeah. Right."

He exhaled a loud sigh over her head, then lowered his gaze and whispered near her ear. She strained to hear him, though why she listened, she wasn't sure.

"I owed Sally a big payoff before November first or the title to Alley Cat went to her. Yes, I didn't have the money I needed. And yes, you solved my problem."

There. Finally the truth.

"But it's not the way you think." She felt the anger slipping away, a heavy sadness taking its place. "It was your *idea* that saved Alley Cat, not your money." She stared at him, the words not making sense.

"I was going to tell you eventually, but..."

Catherine folded her arms across her chest and stared at her tapping foot, afraid of the hope that was beginning to surface.

Jake heaved a loud sigh, then kept his voice low. "My attorney drew up papers separating Alley Cat from Top Cat. This afternoon everything became final. I sold Top Cat to my father, took the money over to Sally's attorney and paid her off."

Catherine looked up at him, eyes brimming. "Why didn't you tell me?" She tried sounding angry but the steam had evaporated.

"Because you would've insisted I take your damn money, that's why?" he said louder. "And my stubborn pride wouldn't let you do it. Okay?"

She reached out to touch his arm, but he withdrew.

"You should have been honest with me," she said feebly, not ready to concede this was *all* her fault.

"And you should have trusted me. I thought you knew me better than anyone."

His words stung more than if he had slapped her. In the background she heard nothing but embarrassed silence. She wished she was the fainting kind, then Jake could carry her out of here and she could tell him what a fool she'd been. Maybe...

Suddenly Jake pulled her into his arms. "I'm sorry, Cat. I've ruined everything, haven't I?" His voice was thick with emotion and she melted against his heaving chest.

"No, Jake." Her voice cracked. "I'm the one who's sorry." She held him tight and didn't move.

From the back of the room came a light tinkling noise, then she heard it again, this time louder. Soon everyone had found a glass and spoon and were tapping out the symbolic sound.

Jake spoke close to her ear. "You know what they want, don't you?"

Catherine stepped back and saw the man she loved, warm and giving, flashing her his best Sam Elliott smile. "I know what I want."

Their lips no sooner met when audible sighs of relief filled the room, followed shortly after by laughter, tears and a fresh round of drinks. Jake kissed Catherine again, bending her backward, playing to the audience.

Suddenly the chatter was deafening as the party continued with renewed vitality. Not until the doorbell rang did the room fall silent again. Seconds later Ellie ushered Uncle Will into the study.

"Sorry I'm late. Did I miss anything?"

Quick glances flitted around the room then everyone exploded into simultaneous laughter.

Mason clasped his brother-in-law's shoulder. "We'll have lunch next week and I'll fill you in. How would you like some champagne and a piece of Catherine's birthday cake?"

"I'd like both, but maybe later. First things first." He moved directly to the couple in front of the fireplace, draping an arm around each of them, and turning their backs to the others.

"Congratulations you two." He looked closely into their eyes, one at a time. "Would you like to wait awhile longer or are we ready to proceed?"

Catherine gazed over at Jake, her throat suddenly dry. "I'm ready if you are."

Jake eyed her for the longest time. Seeming to have lost his tongue, he nodded.

"And you have the license and all?"

Jake patted his pocket and nodded again.

"Good. Well then..." They turned around in unison. He didn't need to ask for silence. The small group had moved closer, suddenly curious.

The judge began in his warm baritone voice. "With the exception of Catherine's parents, and maybe Ellie, I think I've been to more of Catherine's birthday parties than anyone." He looked down at her fondly, squeezing her hand. "I was here when she got her first two-wheel bike. I was even here when she came running in crying with her first skinned knee." He looked at the loved ones who had gathered in front of them and beamed broadly.

"And I'm so very proud to be here tonight—" he glanced one more time at Catherine then Jake "—to join this special couple in Holy Matrimony."

There was a collective intake of air from the shocked faces staring back at them. Catherine's mother was the first to respond.

"Now? Tonight? Oh, Catherine!" She scanned the room nervously, as if searching for a way to postpone the inevitable. "But...but flowers...and...and..." her gaze traveled the length of her daughter's dress. "Catherine...you're wearing black!"

Catherine stepped forward and embraced her. "Mother...I *had* the big white church wedding. It was beautiful and I love you for all your hard work, but—" She looked over her shoulder at Jake whose loving face gave her the confidence to finish. "But all the waiting and decorations and white in the world didn't make me happy in the end." She kissed her mother on the cheek then moved to her father.

His loving embrace said more than his words spoken softly over her shoulder. "More than anything, Catherine, we just want you happy."

At this point, Aunt Helen honked into her hankie and Catherine glanced around. There wasn't a dry eye in the room.

Uncle Will picked up the reins once again. "If Becky and Charlie would stand on either side, I think we can begin."

When the judge finished the short traditional vows, and introduced the new "Mr. and Mrs. Jake Alley" to the small entourage, the applause was long and loud. Finally Uncle Will held up his hands for quiet.

"Do the newlyweds have anything special they'd like to say?"

Catherine found her voice first. "We love you all and we're so happy you could be here with us tonight." She started to sniff and Jake took over.

"Ditto." He waited for the laughter to die down. Then eyeing his new wife he added, "This way I'll never forget your birthday or our anniversary."

Catherine smiled through happy tears. "Don't think this means one gift." Jake pulled her into a tight embrace and kissed her long and hard.

Uncle Will rubbed his hands together. "Now...where's my champagne and chocolate cake?"

Jake and Catherine accepted another round of hugs, kisses and well wishes until the last one left them standing alone in front of the fire.

Jake stepped back from Catherine and gazed down at her tenderly. "What's say we leave and begin our second honeymoon?"

Behind them, Charlie called out, "Where you two going? Can we come along?" Everyone laughed, the earlier tension and champagne obliterating the last of their reserves.

Jake pulled Cat to his side and answered the question. "Cat asked me to surprise her. Then she prized me with questions every chance she got. But I'll tell you this much, whatever we do it will involve a sailboat. Exactly when, where and for how long is still a secret." He looked at his wife and winked.

Catherine's mother looked worried again. "Will you have a crew?"

Cat laughed. "I guess I never told you about..." She almost said "Jamaica," but that was one secret better kept. "Jake's a real seaman," she said, then gazed up at Jake mischievously. "Should I tell them about your boat—*Cat's Meow?*"

"Cat's Meow?" Becky and her parents said in unison, before bursting into laughter.

Jake shot Catherine a hot glare. She hadn't meant to hurt him. She knew how much his boat meant to him.

Then Jake shrugged and the frown disappeared. "I guess it is a silly name. But she was one great boat." His smile was genuine and Catherine was relieved another incident had been averted.

"It's not silly, sweetheart," she said. "It's kind of—"

"I know. Cute." Jake smiled and tugged his bride closer. Together they said their last goodbyes, and a few minutes later stepped out into the biting wind and closed the door.

Catherine felt a wave of excitement that started at her toes and traveled to the ends of her hair, leaving her breathless. She couldn't wait to see Jake's expression when he spotted her gift.

Jake stood in front of the door, gazing into her eyes with such love that she thought she might burst with happiness. Finally he turned and started down the path to the driveway. Two more steps and he froze in place. He squeezed her fingers so hard they hurt.

"Cat! You didn't?"

Behind Jake's Jeep stood *Cat's Meow,* tall and proud. It was covered with a light green tarp, resting on a long flatbed trailer, the rig's engine purring evenly in the cold, still night.

"Oh, yes, I did," she said, a feeling of pure joy rippling through her. "And you're not going to give me a hard time about buying it for you." It was more a statement than a question.

"And if I do?"

She lifted her chin, the answer ready and waiting. "Not too long ago I asked you 'If you won the lottery and bought me something expensive and I refused it, what would you do?' Remember what you said?"

"I'd put you over my knee and spank your butt?"

"My cute little butt, to be precise."

He cupped his hands beneath her bottom and pulled her closer, brushing a light kiss on the tip of her nose. "And cute it is, my beautiful bride."

Catherine looked up at him, the sass disappearing from her eyes. "Then you're not going to give me a hard time?"

He glanced at his treasured boat, then back to her glowing face.

"Mrs. Alley...count on it."

*   *   *   *   *

COMING NEXT MONTH

It's Silhouette Desire's 1000th birthday! Join us for a spectacular three-month celebration, starring your favorite authors and the hottest heroes of the decade!

#997 BABY DREAMS—Raye Morgan
The Baby Shower
Sheriff Rafe Lonewolf couldn't believe his feisty new prisoner was the innocent woman she claimed to be. But a passionate night with Cami Bishop was suddenly making *him* feel criminal!

#998 THE UNWILLING BRIDE—Jennifer Greene
The Stanford Sisters
Paige Stanford's new neighbor was sexy, smart…and single! Little did she know Stefan Michaelovich wanted to make *her* his blushing bride!

#999 APACHE DREAM BRIDE—Joan Elliott Pickart
When Kathy Maxwell purchased a dream catcher, she had no idea she'd soon catch herself an Apache groom! But could her dream really come true…or would she have to give up the only man she ever loved?

#1000 MAN OF ICE—Diana Palmer
Silhouette Desire #1000!
After one tempestuous night with irresistible Barrie Bell, May's MAN OF THE MONTH, Dawson Rutherford, swore off love forever. Now the only way he could get the land he wanted was to make Barrie his temporary bride.

#1001 INSTANT HUSBAND—Judith McWilliams
The Wedding Night
Nick St. Hilarion needed a mother for his daughter, not a woman for himself to love! But when Ann Lennon arrived special delivery, he realized he might not be able to resist falling for his mail-order wife!

#1002 BABY BONUS—Amanda Kramer
Debut Author
Leigh Townsend was secretly crazy about sexy Nick Romano, but she wasn't going to push him to propose! So she didn't tell him he was going to be a daddy—or else he would insist on becoming a husband, too.

SILHOUETTE®
Desire
CELEBRATION 1000

A treasured piece of romance could be yours!

During April, May and June as part of Desire's Celebration 1000 you can enter to win an original piece of art used on an actual Desire cover!

Or you could win one of 300 autographed Man of the Month books!

See Official Sweepstakes Rules for more details.

To enter, complete an Official Entry Form or a 3"x5" card by hand printing "Silhouette Desire Celebration 1000 Sweepstakes", your name and address, and mail to: **In the U.S.:** Silhouette Desire Celebration 1000 Sweepstakes, P.O. Box 9069, Buffalo, N.Y. 14269-9069, or **In Canada:** Silhouette Desire Celebration 1000 Sweepstakes, P.O. Box 637, Fort Erie, Ontario L2A 5X3. Limit one entry per envelope. Entries must be sent via first-class mail and be received no later than 6/30/96. No liability is assumed for lost, late or misdirected mail.

Official Entry Form—Silhouette Desire Celebration 1000 Sweepstakes

Name: _____

Address: _____

City: _____

State/Province: _____

Zip or Postal Code: _____

Favorite Desire Author: _____

Favorite Desire Book: _____

SWEEPS

SILHOUETTE DESIRE® "CELEBRATION 1000" SWEEPSTAKES
OFFICIAL RULES—NO PURCHASE NECESSARY

To enter, complete an Official Entry Form or a 3"x5" card by hand printing "Silhouette Desire Celebration 1000 Sweepstakes," your name and address, and mail it to: In the U.S.: Silhouette Desire Celebration 1000 Sweepstakes, P.O. Box 9069, Buffalo, NY 14269-9069, or In Canada: Silhouette Desire Celebration 1000 Sweepstakes, P.O. Box 637, Fort Erie, Ontario L2A 5X3. Limit one entry per envelope. Entries must be sent via first-class mail and be received no later than 6/30/96. No liability is assumed for lost, late or misdirected mail.

Prizes: Grand Prize—an original painting (approximate value $1500 U.S.);300 Runner-up Prizes—an autographed Silhouette Desire® Book (approximate value $3.50 U.S./$3.99 CAN. each). Winners will be selected in a random drawing (to be conducted no later than 9/30/96) from among all eligible entries received by D.L. Blair, Inc., an independent judging organization whose decision is final.

Sweepstakes offer is open only to residents of the U.S. (except Puerto Rico) and Canada who are 18 years of age or older, except employees and immediate family members of Harlequin Enterprises Ltd., their affiliates, subsidiaries, and all agencies, entities and persons connected with the use, marketing or conduct of this sweepstakes. All federal, state, provincial, municipal and local laws apply. Offer void where prohibited by law. Taxes and/or duties are the sole responsibility of the winners. Any litigation within the province of Quebec respecting the conduct and awarding of prizes may be submitted to the Regie des alcools des courses et des jeux. All prizes will be awarded; winners will be notified by mail. No substitution for prizes is permitted. Odds of winning are dependent upon the number of eligible entries received.

Grand Prize winner must sign and return an Affidavit of Eligibility within 30 days of notification. In the event of noncompliance within this time period, prize may be awarded to an alternate winner. Any prize or prize notification returned as undeliverable may result in the awarding of that prize to an alternate winner. By acceptance of their prize, winners consent to the use of their names, photographs or likenesses for purposes of advertising, trade and promotion on behalf of Harlequin Enterprises Ltd., without further compensation unless prohibited by law. In order to win a prize, residents of Canada will be required to correctly answer a time-limited arithmetical skill-testing question administered by mail.

For a list of winners (available after October 31, 1996) send a separate self-addressed stamped envelope to: Silhouette Desire Celebration 1000 Sweepstakes Winners, P.O. Box 4200, Blair, NE 68009-4200.

> "Motherhood is full of love, laughter
> and sweet surprises. Silhouette's collection
> is every bit as much fun!"
> —Bestselling author **Ann Major**

This May, treat yourself to...

WANTED:

MOTHER

Silhouette's annual tribute to motherhood takes a
new twist in '96 as three sexy single men prepare for
fatherhood—and saying "I Do!" This collection makes
the perfect gift, not just for moms but for all romance
fiction lovers! Written by these captivating authors:

Annette Broadrick
Ginna Gray
Raye Morgan

> "The Mother's Day anthology from Silhouette is the
> highlight of any romance lover's spring!"
> —Award-winning author **Dallas Schulze**

What do women really want to know?

Trust the world's largest publisher of women's fiction to tell you.

HARLEQUIN ULTIMATE GUIDES™

I CAN FIX THAT

A Guide For Women
Who Want To Do It Themselves

This is the only guide a self-reliant woman will ever need to deal with those pesky items that break, wear out or just don't work anymore. Chock-full of friendly advice and straightforward, step-by-step solutions to the trials of everyday life in our gadget-oriented world! So, don't just sit there wondering how to fix the VCR—run to your nearest bookstore for your copy now!

Available this May, at your favorite retail outlet.

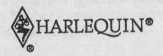

HARLEQUIN®

They're the hardest working, sexiest women in the
Lone Star State...they're

Daughters
OF TEXAS

Annette Broadrick

The O'Brien sisters: Megan, Mollie and Maribeth. Meet them and
the men who want to capture their hearts in these titles from
Annette Broadrick:

MEGAN'S MARRIAGE
(February, Silhouette Desire #979)

The *MAN OF THE MONTH* is getting married to *very* reluctant bride
Megan O'Brien!

INSTANT MOMMY
(March, Silhouette Romance #1139)

A *BUNDLE OF JOY* brings Mollie O'Brien together with the man she's
always loved.

THE GROOM, I PRESUME?
(April, Silhouette Desire #992)

Maribeth O'Brien's been left at the altar—but this bride won't have to
wait long for wedding bells to ring!

Don't miss the DAUGHTERS OF TEXAS—three brides waiting to lasso
the hearts of their very own cowboys! Only from

 **and**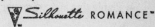

DOT